DISNEP
PIRATES of the CARIBBEAN
LEGENDS OF THE BRETHREN COURT

The Caribbean

Rob Kidd

Based on the earlier adventures of characters created
for the theatrical motion picture,
"Pirates of the Caribbean: The Curse of the Black Pearl"
Screen Story by Ted Elliott & Terry Rossio and
Stuart Beattie and Jay Wolpert,
Screenplay by Ted Elliott & Terry Rossio,
And characters created for the theatrical motion pictures
"Pirates of the Caribbean: Dead Man's Chest" and
"Pirates of the Caribbean: At World's End"
written by Ted Elliott & Terry Rossio

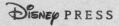

DISNEP PRESS

New York

DISNEY PIRATES OF THE CARIBBEAN

LEGENDS OF THE BRETHREN COURT

The Caribbean

PROLOGUE

A thick, heavy heat hung over the dark jungle. Not a breath of wind stirred the wide leaves or tangled vines, and only slivers of silver moonlight slipped through the dense tree cover.

And yet, despite the stillness . . . something was moving. A ripple of shadow here, a spot of deeper darkness there. And if there had been anyone to watch from the corner of his eye, that someone might have followed this trail of glimmers and half-seen spirits all the way to a house hidden in the darkest of the myriad patches of shadow.

The stones of the house seemed out of place, more suited to Europe than this Caribbean island. There was real glass in the windows, which were thick and warped, but there was nothing to be seen through them; black velvet curtains were drawn tightly, keeping even the smallest flicker of firelight from escaping.

But if the unseen watcher had made it this far through the thick jungle with his sanity intact, he might have peeked through the open door and seen the most terrifying part of this unsettling house: its inhabitant. The man leaned over a long wooden table that nearly filled the front room. Strewn across its surface were strange, arcane objects: beakers of bubbling gold liquid; weights and miniature scales; tiny nonhuman skulls; and sheets and sheets of parchment crowded with ink. Frantic scribblings filled every corner of the pages with indecipherable formulas and notations.

This was the secret laboratory of the Shadow Lord. He was the greatest alchemist the Seven Seas had ever known and the fiercest pirate in the Caribbean . . . and no one knew it but him.

But all that was going to change—starting tonight.

His hands flickered oddly in the candlelight, as if shadows had woven themselves around his palms. His cold eyes peered into the depths of the cauldron on the table in front of him, reflecting the eerie blue light that glowed from the liquid inside.

Slowly, the liquid swirled, and the Shadow Lord raised his hands, twisting the ring on his left middle finger. Images began to form, and in a moment a scene had appeared in the cauldron.

He smiled grimly. Smoke billowed from blazing fires below the full moon. Screams were still rising from the burning fort, and bodies lay scattered across the sand, cut down by his army as they tried to escape.

But nobody would escape. Nobody would live to tell the tale of what had happened here. All that would remain were the destruction, the ruins, the ashes, and the death. It would be as if an army had risen out of the shadows and destroyed everything, then vanished back into the shadows.

He chuckled. That was *exactly* what had happened.

That was how his shadow army worked: the shadows took over any inanimate objects they came across, turning them into deadly, unstoppable, invincible fighters. How was anyone supposed to fight a man made of a chest, with barrels for legs and cannons for arms? Or a monstrous creature of ropes and swords, slicing and weaving like a thing out of their nightmares, with no eyes to gouge, no body to stab, no heart to cut out—nothing to kill?

That was the genius of his shadow army. No need for mere men of flesh and blood, who would either die pathetically or betray you in the end.

"First Panama," he muttered. "Teach them the lesson they should have learned long ago. And then . . . the rest of the world."

The scene in the cauldron shifted, and he smiled wider and wider with each image of the carnage his power had wrought. He caught a glimpse of the ocean beyond and leaned forward suddenly, making an abrupt motion with his hand. Slowly, his view within the cauldron panned out, and he could see the wide, unbroken stretch of sea that lay beside this beach, the waves lapping placidly at the shore as if they were used to witnessing such bloodshed every day.

Then the Shadow Lord's smile fell. Something

was wrong. Terribly wrong. He clenched his fist and slammed the table, sending a cascade of papers and books crashing to the floor.

Gone. His ship was *gone*!

After all the trouble he'd gone through to get a ship, his shadow army had destroyed it on its very first mission. Now, as he swung his view back through the town, he could see pieces of it in the wreckage—a tattered sail here, a broken spar there, the basket of the crow's nest now guttering into ashes on a thatched roof.

Cursed shadow army. He still hadn't figured out quite how to control them the way he meant to. He could raise them, send them forth, and summon them back, but while they were running loose they did idiotic things like take his ship apart to create more warriors. He needed more practice before he'd be ready for his day of vengeance, but that date was approaching quickly.

Swearing murderously, he picked up one of the tiny skulls from his desk and crushed it between his meaty hands. A good thing he hadn't gone to Panama along with the shadow army, as he'd originally planned. If he had, he'd now be stranded there, just waiting for someone to come discover the burned town. How ignominious. How the other pirates would laugh if they knew. Those who remembered him at all already thought he was an incompetent buffoon.

He ground the shards of the skull into dust in his palms, remembering the injustice done to him long ago. Little did the Pirate Lords know that he was still out here, planning his revenge. Even if they did know, they wouldn't worry. "Oh, him," they'd say. "He was a terrible pirate! Could barely stand upright on a ship! Nothing to fear from him."

But they were wrong. They were very, very wrong. And in just about two months, they would find out how wrong they were.

Soon, he thought, the day will come that I've been waiting for for so long. Very soon.

But first he needed a new ship. Perhaps he could steal one from a Pirate Lord. That would be beautifully ironic.

He curled his fingers over the cauldron, and the shadows came rushing back to the Shadow Lord here in his dark house among the jungle vines. As they poured forth, the brooms and buckets and odds and ends of broken wood that the Shadow Army had imbued with life fell to the ground, harmless once more. No one who found the wrecked town would ever know that these innocuous-looking everyday objects were the very instruments of all the death and destruction left behind.

The Shadow Army boiled up from the town into a massive dark cloud that flowed into the sky and seemingly evaporated before reemerging in the cauldron of the Shadow Lord, where it poured out and flooded back into his ring, vanishing. The large stone in the ring slowly turned from crystal clear to pitch black as the shadowy cloud disappeared into it.

Scowling, the Shadow Lord drew his cape around him and went to the door, peering out into the hot, soundless night. Only one thing could calm him when thoughts of revenge and anger threatened to overwhelm him: looking at the source of his power and remembering that he was the only one who possessed it.

Satisfied that no one was lurking in the darkness (no one would ever *want* to lurk in that darkness), the Shadow Lord knelt beside his fireplace and pried up a loose floorboard. He reached into the space underneath and drew out the chest that was hidden there.

But even as he lifted it, his shriveled heart gave an unsteady lurch. It was too light . . . far lighter than usual. Quickly he set it on the floor and flung it open.

Empty.

The vials of Shadow Gold were gone, all seven of them.

Enraged, he leaped to his feet and flung the chest out the window with supernatural strength. The glass shattered and the curtain was torn from the railing. It fluttered like a lost ghost as it fell into the jungle with the chest.

That was *his* Shadow Gold. He had tirelessly labored over it; he had studied for years to figure out how to find the precise combination of liquid gold and orichalcum. He was the one who had found the last supply of orichalcum in the world and measured each painstaking drop into the vials. There was no more; there would never be any other Shadow Gold. He alone knew its power, and he hadn't even discovered the limits of it yet.

But if no one else knew the power contained in the vials, then why would someone want them? They looked like nothing more than small vials of golden liquid with shiny metal flakes in them.

Someone must know. They knew where to find the vials, and they might even know how to use their power—power that could make the thief as strong as the Shadow Lord himself.

Seven vials. Out there in the world.

Who had dared to steal from him? And how?

His mind reeled, and then, focusing, his eyes narrowed. The Pirate Lords of the Brethren Court. If they were behind this . . . especially that most vile of all pirates, Jack Sparrow . . . they would die even more slowly and painfully than the Shadow Lord had first planned.

CHAPTER ONE

"Jack!"

The sun shone merrily on the sparkling blue sea, and the crisp black sails and gleaming, scrubbed decks of the *Black Pearl*. Up at the prow of the ship, a dashing pirate stood proudly, arms akimbo and legs braced against the rolling waves, his dark hair flying in the wind. He turned his head slightly and grinned, letting the sunlight sparkle grandly off his gold tooth.

"JACK!" the voice behind him said again, exasperated.

Jack Sparrow still did not respond. He tried a different way of tilting his head, setting his hat at a jaunty new angle.

The barrel of a pistol poked him forcefully in the ribs.

"I don't know what you're playing at," his first mate snarled from the other end of the pistol, "but I *know* you can hear me, Jack."

"Oh, sorry," Jack said, spinning around with a little wave of his hand. "I presumed you must be addressing some *other* Jack, one who was not captain of the finest ship ever to sail the Seven Seas—since *surely* if you were addressing *me*, you would have said 'Captain Jack,' isn't that right?"

His first mate, his scraggly red beard quivering, heaved a deep, irritated sigh. "My apologies, *Captain* Jack."

"That's much better," Jack said, tapping him lightly on the head. "When we get our new crew in Tortuga, they'll be looking to you for how to behave. Savvy?" He sauntered back toward center deck, then turned, squinting, as a thought struck him. "Oh, and really? Ostrich feathers, Barbossa? Don't you think that's a little much?"

Hector Barbossa narrowed his eyes as Captain Jack Sparrow sashayed along the deck. Barbossa self-consciously touched his new hat, resplendent with enormous ostrich feathers. "We're a-coming up on Tortuga now, *sir*," he called.

"Excellent," Jack called back. "Let's see if we can find some *real* pirates there."

The few remaining crew members glared at him.

"I mean, in addition to you fine . . . swarthy . . . er, burly ruffians," Jack added.

It was surprising how fickle pirates could be. One tiny misadventure—one mislabeled treasure map, one chest of mold instead of gold—and they scattered to the winds, grumbling and muttering and throwing dark glances back at their dashing captain. As if it were his fault! So what if he was the one who'd bought the map? Any other pirate captain would have done the same at that ridiculously low price.

Well, no matter. If there was one thing that was easy to find in the Caribbean, it was a fresh supply of pirates. With his loyal first mate, Barbossa, at his side, Jack would sweep into Tortuga and no doubt the best pirates would fall all over themselves to join him.

They only had to take one look at his magnificent ship to see the advantages of being part of Jack's crew. The *Black Pearl*! Fastest ship in the Caribbean! This was a far cry from his first command, the lowly *Barnacle*.* Pirates dreamed

---

* Jack's adventures aboard the *Barnacle* are chronicled in the 12-volume book series, Jack Sparrow.

all their lives of having a ship like the *Pearl*, and now it was his: risen from the depths of Davy Jones's Locker.

And all he had to do to get it was barter away his soul. Jack straightened his hat, brushing away the uneasiness that came with that thought. He didn't have to worry about his bargain for another thirteen years. He'd find a way to deal with it by then. For now, he had thirteen years of freedom to look forward to—thirteen years of freedom with his loyal crew and his splendid ship.

But first, he had to find that loyal crew.

Tortuga was as crowded and loud and vile as ever. From the wharf, Jack could see the Faithful Bride tavern, where he had met his original first mate, Arabella Smith,* so many years ago. He

---

* In *Jack Sparrow*, Vol. 1, *The Coming Storm*.

knew she wasn't there anymore. He'd be lucky to find any pirates with half her courage and intelligence.

Jack strolled down the gangplank as his paltry crew scurried about, tying up the boat.

"Oh, Jaaack," Barbossa said, leaning over the railing above.

Jack raised an eyebrow at him.

"I mean, *Captain* Jack," Barbossa said, rolling his eyes. "Why don't I stay here with the ship? I can . . . keep an eye on things. While you're gone." He smiled ingratiatingly. "Trust me, I'll take good care of the *Pearl*."

"Nonsense," Jack said. "I need your keen eye and sound judgment in choosing a crew, Barbossa. A noble offer, but I insist you accompany me to the Faithful Bride."

Barbossa scowled. "Very well, then," he said, stomping down the gangplank to join Jack.

But Jack was distracted by the sight of a

familiar face at the end of the dock.

"Bill!" he cried in delight, dashing up to his old friend. "Billy Turner? Is it really you?"

"Oh, hello, Jack," Billy said in his usual serious way. "I wondered if I would see you here sooner or later."

"But this is marvelous!" Jack exclaimed, seizing Bill's hand and pumping it up and down. "This is your lucky day, old friend! It just so happens that due to surprising and unforeseen circumstances entirely beyond my control, there is a position available with my crew."

One of Jack's crew stormed past, flinging an end of rope at Jack. "Tie up yer own cursed ship!" he snapped. "I'm off to find a ship whose cap'n ain't barmy as a seagull."

"Perhaps *more* than one position, then," Jack amended, throwing his arm around Bill's shoulder. "Know anyone else who might want to join us? Perchance that fellow we once sailed with, what was his name? Oh, yes—Owbout Yew?"

"Yew?" Billy asked, perplexed. He had known Jack for years but couldn't always understand his quick wit. Then Bill's curious expression deflated upon realizing what Jack was suggesting. "Oh, '*you*,' not 'yew.' Not you, me. I mean, you want me to join your crew. Thanks, Jack, flattered," Billy said, pulling himself away from Jack, "but I'm not looking for work. I'm just trying to get home."

"But Billy, lad!" Jack protested. "Take a look at my ship!" He gestured grandiosely toward the *Pearl*. "The *Black Pearl*, Billy—remember the stories we used to hear about the fastest ship in the world? This is it! But it's even faster now."

"Not faster than Davy Jones's ship, the *Flying Dutchman*," Billy said gloomily.

"Pfft," Jack said with a dismissive wave. "Unfair advantage. Extrasupernatural, dead crew, all that. Also, did you notice my hat? Isn't it excellent? Come on, Bill—we're going to have grand adventures!"

"Pirate adventures, you mean," Bill said. "No thanks, Jack. I have responsibilities now."

"Yes," Jack said disapprovingly, narrowing his kohl-lined eyes. "And how is the little wife?"

"She's doing very well, Jack," Bill said. "I know she'd love for you to visit. And then you could meet our son."

"Your *what*?" Jack said, cupping his hand behind his ear. "Come again?"

"Our son, Jack—we have a baby boy."

"Oh," said Jack with little interest. He looked around the bustling wharf as if hoping something would happen to change the subject. Then a thought occurred to him. "Did you name him Jack, by any chance?"

Bill chuckled. "I'm afraid not, Jack. He's a William, like me."

"Oh," Jack said, losing interest again. "I just

thought you might want to name him after your mentor and role model . . . the greatest pirate captain in the Caribbean . . . someone who's always been a friend to you *and* that bonnie lass of yours . . . no, no, that's all right." He paused. "Saved your lives on a number of occasions, I did," Jack turned the dagger a little more. "Oh, well, maybe the next one?" he said hopefully.

"Maybe," Bill agreed with a smile.

"Well, 'William' shouldn't stop you from having a bit of an adventure before going home," Jack said. "Wouldn't you like to take some pirate gold back to your baby-who-is-not-named-Jack?"

"I left to make my fortune on a merchant ship," Bill said glumly, "but we were attacked by Spanish pirates not far from here, and they stole the ship. I've been stranded on Tortuga ever since."

"Spanish pirates!" Jack scoffed. "Vagabonds and lummoxes! What are they doing in *our*

Caribbean, I'd like to know? Don't they have their own sea to pillage and plunder? It seems like all you hear about nowadays are Spanish pirates. When people really should be talking about me instead."

"Well, they're none too friendly, that's for certain," Bill said.

"You know what you should do," Jack said sagely. "You should stash that kid of yours in an orphanage. Or a monastery. Happens to boys all the time, and lots of them grow up to be terrific pirates. Then you and the missus can come on a little jaunt with me—liberate some treasure, get some fresh sea air, maybe even an excellent hat of your own. The kid'll be there when you get back. Trust me, he won't even notice you've gone."

"No, Jack," Bill said firmly.

"Freedom!" Jack cried, waving his arms madly. "The wind in your hair! Rum! Salty wenches! Sea air!" He paused, thinking for a minute. "Did I mention rum?"

"I'm going home," Bill insisted, setting his jaw. "That's all I want—to get back home."

Jack eyed him shrewdly from head to toe. A plan was forming in his mind. A plan to keep Billy with him long enough to persuade him to join the *Pearl*. "Home, eh?" he said. "And where is home these days?"

"North Carolina," Bill said, tipping his head to the north. "Not many boats going all that way, I'm afraid."

Jack rubbed his chin thoughtfully, twisting the braids of his beard. "Hmmm," he said. "Tell you what, Billy, my friend. Why don't we give you a lift?"

Bill eyed him with deep suspicion. "All the way to North Carolina?"

"Why not?" Jack said, spreading his hands. "We've got nowhere else to be. We might as well venture up the coast and see how things are. Then we can drop you off and be on our merry way, eh?"

"And what do *you* get out of it?" Bill asked.

Jack looked injured. He pressed one hand to his heart and had the most innocent expression on his face. "Why, I get to spend some quality time with one of my very good friends," he said.

Bill still looked dubious.

"And I hear there's treasure in the Carolina islands," Jack tried.

"Ah," Bill said, relaxing. "Well, that makes more sense. If you're sure you'd be going that way anyway."

"Of course!" Jack said. "With the speed of my fine ship, we'll have you home in no time at all." He smiled, showing all his teeth. It had been a very long time since Bill had seen Jack. He'd forgotten what that smile meant—that Jack might not exactly be telling the whole truth.

"Thanks, Jack," Bill said with a tight, forced grin. "I appreciate it."

"We just have to stop by the tavern and pick up a few pirates before we go," Jack said. "Barbossa!" he yelled. He turned and saw his first mate frozen halfway up the gangplank, as if he'd been sneaking back on board. "Come on, Hector, stop dawdling!" Jack called. "What's taking you so long? We have pirates to recruit!"

Clapping Bill on the back, he steered his friend into the crowd. With a muttered curse, Barbossa trailed behind them up the hill to the Faithful Bride.

A pair of eyes watched, unseen, as the three pirates swaggered away from the *Black Pearl*. The watcher had heard every word Jack said. The fastest ship in the Caribbean? That was exactly what he needed. . . .

The hidden figure snuck closer to the ship,

eyeing the scruffy pirates who'd been left to guard it. One was picking his nails with his sword. The other was leaning sleepily on a barrel, his eyes drooping. Neither paid any attention to the splash in the water behind them. Neither noticed the ship bob a little in the water as someone grabbed a rope on the other side and hauled himself up and over the railing.

Not a single pirate on the *Black Pearl* had any idea that someone had snuck onto their ship. Nobody saw him slip quietly belowdecks and disappear into the shadows of the hold.

CHAPTER TWO

Even in the middle of the day, the Faithful Bride was crowded with cutthroats, drunken louts, and scoundrels in search of a ship to join (or steal, or loot). The sounds of singing and bottles smashing drifted out to Jack and his partners as they approached the rundown shack. Soon they were hit by its familiar smell of seaweed and wet wood and ale and fish. Mostly ale. Pirates often joked that so many pints had been spilled at the Faithful Bride that the floorboards were now more ale than wood.

Inside the door, the three men paused to let their eyes adjust to the candlelight; only splinters of sunshine peeked through the cracks in the window shutters. Several unsavory characters eyed them in a rather unfriendly way, but Jack casually adjusted his coat so they could see the sword at his waist, and they turned back to their tankards, muttering unpleasantly.

"All right, lads," Jack announced. Some of the drinkers stopped singing to peer at him groggily. "Who here would like to join the finest pirate crew ever to sail the Caribbean?"

"Why, is Villanueva hiring?" one of them called, and a few others laughed.

Jack sniffed. Villanueva was a Pirate Lord— the Spanish one—and he was *supposed* to be on the other side of the Atlantic, bothering (and stealing from) Spaniards. Not here, competing with Jack for fame and attention.

"You would be joining the *Black Pearl*. You may have heard of it by its former name, the *Wicked Wench*," he said, grinning at the whispers that ran around the room. People had heard of his ship, all right. Several of them stood up to approach him. "And you would be sailing under the command of the famous Pirate Lord of the Caribbean, *Captain* Jack Sparrow!"

Everybody sat down again, clearly deflated.

"Oh, come now," Jack said. "It's all slander and calumny! Don't believe everything you hear! Well, maybe *most* things. But it's going to be different this time, me hearties. Treasure and fortune await!"

All the drinkers stared fixedly into their mugs of ale.

"Well," Jack said. "We are going to sit down right over here, and you can all line up to be interviewed." He sat down with a flourish at one of the empty wooden tables and waited for a long moment. "No pushing," he added. "Let's be civilized."

"This is embarrassing," Barbossa hissed, pulling up a chair beside Jack. "Let's just go somewhere else."

"Nonsense," Jack said, waving his hand. "Why, here comes a likely candidate now."

The man weaving tipsily up to their table looked on the young side for a pirate. He wore pointed boots that slipped and slid on the sticky, ale-covered floorboards. His belt held a holster, but no pistols. The green bandanna around his neck sure looked as if it was covered in tiny daisies. And his too-big hat kept sliding down over his eyes.

Barbossa snorted. " 'Likely candidate'? Likely to fall overboard the moment the ship moves, if you ask me."

"Oh, let's give him a chance," Bill said.

At the last minute, the ungainly stranger tripped, apparently on nothing, and half-fell, half-collapsed into the chair in front of them. All three of them leaned forward and examined him.

"And what makes you think you're worthy to crew the *Black Pearl*?" Jack asked him, signaling for a bottle of rum.

"Um," the stranger stammered. "I like . . . boats? No, seagulls. No, boats. Wait—both!"

"Perfect," Jack said. "Enthusiasm. I like it."

Barbossa put his head in his hands and sighed deeply.

"You've made an excellent choice," Jack said, beaming at the stranger. "There is no finer ship in the Caribbean—nay, the world."

"Name?" Barbossa barked.

"Catastrophe Shane," the man said awkwardly, tipping his hat at them, then pushing it back again as it fell over his eyes.

"Catastrophe Shane!" Jack cried with glee. "I've never heard a better fearsome pirate name! Other than Captain Jack Sparrow, of course."

Barbossa rolled his eyes.

"I can see there's no need to ask you any questions," Jack sailed on. "With a name like Catastrophe Shane, you must be a truly ferocious, bloodthirsty, dangerous pirate."

Billy noticed that Catastrophe Shane was turning a little green.

"I bet you don't carry pistols because you can't trust your merciless nature, is that it?" Jack guessed. "You know how fierce and hot-tempered you are, and you're resisting temptation by leaving them at home."

"Um . . ." said Shane.

"Perfect!" Jack said. "You'll fit right in on the *Pearl.* Make your mark here." He slid a parchment across the table to Catastrophe Shane.

"Jack!" Barbossa protested.

"*Captain* Jack," Jack reminded him. "And as the captain, what I say goes. Welcome aboard, Catastrophe Shane."

Barbossa narrowed his eyes again. "Very well," he said. "But you must get rid of that ridiculous hat."

Jack nodded. "Yes, I'm afraid we can't have any hats more dramatic than mine."

"Oh—all right," said Shane, taking it off and turning it in his hands with a bewildered expression.

Jack leaned forward and added in a loud whisper, "Barbossa thinks his hat outshines mine because of the ostrich feathers, but everyone knows that it just makes his head look like the ratty nest of a dead bird."

Barbossa glared at him.

Another stranger sidled up as Shane went to stand behind Billy. This one was older and quite a bit more rotund, with a long, drooping, fat brown moustache. He winked a lot as he talked and constantly fiddled with his hands, but he seemed friendly—a little *too* friendly for a pirate, but Jack and his nascent crew couldn't exactly be picky.

"I'm Henry," he said, introducing himself. "Are you really the great Captain Jack Sparrow?"

"I most certainly am," Jack said, beaming again. "Unless he owes you money. In which case, no, never heard of him."

"I've heard so much about you," Henry said. "Aren't you one of the youngest Pirate Lords the Brethren Court has ever had?"

Jack pretended to blush. "Well, I don't like to brag," he said. Then he steadied himself. Yes, I'm the youngest captain ever to become a Pirate Lord."

"Even from the second court?" Henry asked. "What about Morgan and Bartholomew?

The ones who wrote the Code? I thought I heard . . ."

"Oh, *that* court," Jack said dismissively. "Nobody remembers *that* court. What's important is who's a Pirate Lord *now*. For instance, me."

"Well, I'd be honored to sail with you, Captain," Henry said, "if you'll have me." He offered his hand to Jack, and Jack shook it, looking extremely pleased with himself.

"Certainly," he said. "I always trust a man with a good firm handshake like that. We'd be deli—"

"PIRATES!" boomed a voice from the doorway. A surprisingly short, bearded man stood framed in the light from outside, decked out in a well-worn leather coat with fountains of Spanish lace at his throat and cuffs. His wide-brimmed hat was adorned with feathers, and his weathered brown skin indicated his age, as did the streaks of gray in his black beard and moustache. "VAGABONDS! MEN OF THE SEA!" he bellowed.

Jack scowled. He would recognize that lilting foreign accent anywhere. It was the Spanish Pirate Lord Villanueva. He dropped Henry's hand and rose to his feet.

"Ahoy there, Captain Noisy," he said, "some of us are trying to conduct business in here. Civilized business, with no shouting."

Villanueva ignored him. "I am in need of a few strong men for my crew," he said. Two very large, very burly pirates stepped up behind him and crossed their arms. Jack started examining his dirty nails with deep interest.

The Spanish Pirate Lord drew his sword. "You," he said, pointing with it to a well-muscled sailor near the door. "And you. And you." He selected a few more of the strongest, least smelly, most sober candidates. Then he paused and looked around. His gaze fell on Jack's little gathering. He gave a small, sinister laugh. "And you," he said, pointing his sword tip directly at Henry's squidgy midsection.

"You can't have him! He's mine, I say!" Jack protested.

"I did agree to . . ." Henry began weakly. The Spaniard poked him lightly in the belly.

"I said YOU," Villanueva declared with finality. "Out. The *Centurion* is leaving now." The other pirates who had been chosen stood and began to file out of the bar without arguing.

Henry gave Jack a helpless look. Jack was debating whether to start a sword fight with Villanueva right there in the tavern when the Spaniard's two burly companions stepped forward and loomed menacingly over him.

"Ah, well," Jack said to Henry. "It was a terrific partnership while it lasted. And I hear the weather is lovely in Spain."

One of the big pirates firmly took Henry's arm and escorted him from the room. Villanueva tipped his hat to Jack with a sardonic smile and sauntered out, taking all the best pirates in the room with him.

"And *that*," Barbossa said pointedly to Jack, "is how it's done." He took a swig from one of the tankards of ale that the barkeeper had brought them.

"Typical arrogant Spaniards," Jack observed, sitting down again. "As if the East India Trading Company isn't trouble enough, now we have to deal with the regular Spanish navy everywhere *and* Spanish pirates as well." He shook his head mournfully. "Why can't the Caribbean just be full of mermaids and vengeful ghosts and shape-shifting sorceresses? I ask you. *Those* I know how to deal with." He reached for his glass and discovered that it was empty. "Hey, why is the rum gone?"

Billy carefully didn't look at Catastrophe Shane, who hiccupped innocently. "You were right not to start a fight with them," Billy said. "Villanueva would chase you all the way around the world if he thought you'd offended him or taken something he wanted."

"He'd never catch the *Pearl*!" Jack said jauntily. "Well, it's not all bad news." He clapped Shane on the back. "At least we have Catastrophe Shane!"

CHAPTER THREE

"This is a disaster," Barbossa said.

"I wouldn't say *disaster*," said Jack, wrinkling his forehead expressively.

"Oh, really?" Barbossa said. "Would you say . . . catastrophe?"

Another crash came from the bow of the ship, where Catastrophe Shane was trying to rig a sail but kept falling over his boots. They'd given him a pistol earlier so he could take target practice, and then they'd taken it right back after he shot a barrel of ale, the ocean, and the air above a very startled seagull.

"Maybe you should practice later," Jack had suggested warily.

Now, as the *Pearl* sailed out of Tortuga's harbor, the captain and first mate watched Catastrophe Shane stagger from one side of the boat to the other, getting tangled in the rope. The other pirates were staring at him in open-mouthed disbelief.

"He's just getting his sea legs," Jack said. "Nothing to worry about."

Barbossa shook his head. "I am pleased to point out, as I so often do," he said, "that I told you so."

Jack put his hand on his chest, frowning. It felt like something heavy had suddenly sat on his heart—as if an enormous weight was now slowly pressing down on his chest.

"Did it just get colder?" he asked, glancing up at the fiercely burning sun. But despite the sun's heat, to Jack it felt as if freezing darkness was creeping over him.

"No," Barbossa said, peering at him curiously. "Why? Are you feeling poorly? How poorly? Deathly poorly, perhaps?"

"No, no," Jack said. "Just a bit of a chill. Thank you for your concern."

Barbossa looked disappointed.

Billy came striding along the deck toward them. "There's something odd about this ship, Jack," he said. "I could have sworn someone was watching me while I inspected the hold."

"Piffle," Jack said. "All our fine pirates are up here, sailing the ship."

"Also our *less* fine pirates," Barbossa muttered.

Jack blinked, putting his hand on his chest again. This was really quite odd. "I'll be in my cabin," he said, taking a step toward the hatch.

"Oh, *Cap-tain*," Barbossa said. "Aren't you forgetting something?"

"Am I?" Jack said. He was having trouble concentrating. It seemed as if there were darkness at the edges of his sight, like fog rolling in from either side—but when he turned his head, the sun shone as brightly and the sea sparkled as merrily in every direction, just as they had before.

"Where are we going?" Barbossa asked. "Our bearing? Care to give an order, *Captain*?"

"Oh," Jack said, taking another step. "North Carolina, I suppose. Make sail and all that. You know the drill."

Billy looked delighted. It hadn't been a trick after all! He took the wheel from Barbossa as Jack walked slowly to the captain's cabin.

"Is he all right?" Billy asked the first mate.

Barbossa smiled sinisterly, watching Jack's slow, weaving steps. "We shall see."

Jack was not all right. After a moment at his desk, he stood up and went to lie down on the couch, closing his eyes. How unpleasant it was to be sick. Unpleasant and unusual. Jack Sparrow never felt ill a day in his life.

"Snap out of it, man," he told himself briskly. He sat up, got to his feet, wobbled unsteadily, and sat down again. His whole chest felt as if it had been filled with anchors—dark, mossy anchors that had dragged among the shadows of the deepest ocean. It was hard to breathe with this weight on his heart.

Something darted across the corner of the room and he leaped to his feet, drawing his sword.

"Who's there?" he challenged loudly. "Show yourself!"

No one emerged. All he could see now were shadows. He strode over to the corner and poked all the shadows vigorously with his sword, but there was nothing there. He spun around again.

"You don't want to annoy Captain Jack Sparrow!" he shouted, charging to the other side of the room and stabbing the wall with his sword.

Not a sound, but as he turned again, he thought he caught a glimpse of something winding between his feet. With a gasp, he jumped back and stabbed the floor . . . but there was nothing there.

"Am I seeing shadow cats now?" he muttered. "Or perhaps I'm still haunted by that mangy furball, Constance." On his earlier adventures, Jack had traveled with a boy named Jean Magliore, who claimed his sister Constance had been turned into a cat by the mystic, Tia Dalma. Although she was the most irritating, ugly feline Jack had ever seen, Jean doted on her with a ridiculous amount of affection.

"Leave me alone!" Jack yelled, flailing wildly at the shadows and anything else he could see. "I don't like cats! I don't like anchors in my chest!

I want none of any of this! Away with you!"

He paused, breathing hard. Was that a sound? *Knock, knock, knock.*

Ah. He threw open the door.

The entire crew of the *Pearl* was gathered outside his cabin, staring at him. Billy, who had been the one knocking, took a step back when he saw Jack's pale, furious face.

"Er . . . you all right, Jack?" Billy asked.

"Perfectly," Jack said nonchalantly, straightening his hat. "You?"

Billy leaned over and peeked past Jack at the cabin, which was now a huge mess, with chairs overturned and papers scattered in all directions. "Um . . . we just . . . heard some noise in here."

"Nothing at all," Jack said airily. "Just your brave captain thinking hard." He tapped his forehead knowingly. "Making plans. Piratical plans. As you do."

"Oh . . . sure," Billy said.

The rest of the crew exchanged glances. Well, Jack thought, all the best pirate captains are a little mad. It'll be good for my reputation.

Something tugged on one of the beads in his hair, and he whipped his head around, glaring. But, of course, there was nothing there. Now he could feel more tugging, on his coat and his boots and his sword, but wherever he looked, there was nothing.

No. Captain Jack Sparrow might *act* mad, but he would never actually *be* mad. This was something foul and unnatural. This illness had not just *happened.*

Someone had cursed him.

He marched past the gaping pirates. "Back to work!" he called over his shoulder, and he heard the clump of their boots as they went.

At the wheel, Barbossa beamed at him. "Strain of command too much for you, Jack? Maybe you need a rest. A *long* rest."

"No, no," Jack said. "But we're changing course."

"Oh?" Barbossa said.

"Set sail for the Pantano River," Jack said.

There was one person who knew more about curses than anyone else. Of course, she was usually the one casting them . . . but hopefully that wasn't the case this time. He had to hope that she'd know how to free him from this mysterious illness.

He was going to see Tia Dalma.

CHAPTER FOUR

Jack was standing at the railing, looking out to sea and trying to breathe normally while ignoring all the shadows darting in the corners of his vision. He glanced sideways and saw Billy Turner come on deck. Billy looked up at the sun and frowned. He pulled out his pocket watch and checked it. Then he turned as if gauging the angle of the sun to figure out in which direction they were going. Pretty soon, he would discern that it was *not* in the direction of North Carolina.

Jack hightailed it into the hold. Billy wouldn't think to look for him down there. By the time he found the captain, they'd be well on their way to Tia Dalma's shack.

The cargo hold was vast and dark and unfortunately quite a bit emptier than Jack liked, what with not having any treasure chests or piles of gold in it. He'd forgotten to bring a light, but perhaps that was for the best. A candle would only create more shadows, moving and leaping. Now everything was one big, still shadow, and he could sit in the dark, brooding and hidden.

The tugging on his hair and beard and clothes was still going on, but now that he'd decided it was supernatural and invisible, it was easier to ignore. He felt his way over to a pile of crates and perched on top with a sigh.

Behind him, something moved in the dark.

Something not so invisible . . . but Jack didn't notice it. He rested his chin on his hand and wondered where this illness could have come from and who had cursed him. It seemed a bit unfair. He caused himself enough supernatural trouble without a mysterious someone adding to it.

Jack, whispered a voice in his head. "Oh, no, you don't," Jack said forcefully. "It isn't bad enough that I'm seeing things, I have to *hear* them, too? Enough muttering, shadows. Out of my head!"

Witty Jack . . . I be not one of your shadows. . . .

Jack frowned. Only one person called him "witty Jack."

"Tia Dalma?" he said.

Clever, clever Jack . . .

"Well, this is convenient," Jack said. "You being in my head and all. I was just on my way to see you. Very obliging of you to turn up here instead. Go ahead and appear, if you like—you know you're always welcome here. Er, within reason."

No, Jack. It is best, you coming to see me. I have t'ings to show you . . . t'ings you must see and do. . . .

"Madam, I don't do *t'ings* for anybody but myself," Jack pointed out.

This definitely be for yourself, witty Jack.

"Ah," Jack said, "well, in that case, not a problem. We'll be there in a heartbeat. Some supernatural winds would be helpful, if you'd like to contribute."

I be not at the Pantano River bayou, witty Jack. The glittering city awaits you; go there and seek me upriver.

"What?" Jack protested, irritated. "Why can't you just be where I want to find you? Why do I have to solve a riddle to get there? Why can't you just come *here*?"

Jack . . . the world is not always arranged for your liking alone.

"So what's the glittering city, then?" Jack said. He thought for a moment. "Last glittering city I saw was New Orleans. 'Course, it was glittering because it was made of silver, which some may say was my fault. Which it was. A little. Well, a lot my fault. But I fixed it, so I don't see what they're going on about.*"

No response from the voice in his head.

"New Orlcans?" Jack guessed sheepishly.

See you soon, witty Jack. . . .

"I'll take that as a yes, then," Jack said. The voice did not speak again. He shook his head, batting away the invisible creatures that were tugging at his hair and trying to steal his excellent hat. "I'll have you know," Jack said pointedly to his tormentors, "you dread fiends

---

* In *Jack Sparrow*, Vols. 5, 6, and 7, *The Age of Bronze, Silver,* and *City of Gold.*

of the dark, that I am not afraid of you. Not even remotely. You see, unlike Tia Dalma, I know that *you* don't really exist, so—"

As he spoke, he reached behind him to see if there were any rum bottles in the cubbyholes along the wall. And then his hand hit something. Something warm. And alive.

Something that said: *"Madre de Dios!"*

"AAAAAAAAAAAAAAAAAAAAAAAAAAAAA AAAAAAAAH!!!!!!!!!!!" Jack howled, launching himself to his feet.

"AAAAAAAAAAAAAAAAAAAAAAAAAAAAA AAAAAAAAH!!!!!!!!!!!" shrieked the thing in the dark.

"You *are* real!" Jack shouted, spinning and flailing at the darkness. "I knew it! Scoundrel! Cur! I'll have your bones for earrings! Or, no, that would be rather disgusting and not at all attractive. Stand and fight!" He wrestled with his sword, but it was caught in one of the crates.

"Please, señor! Please forgive me!" the other voice cried.

Boots thundered down the stairs and several pirates charged into the hold, waving torches and lanterns. The bright glow of the light fell on a boy cowering in front of Jack.

He was young—probably sixteen, about the age Jack had been when he set out on his first adventures aboard the *Barnacle*. His dark hair was disheveled and matted with straw, his eyes were brown, wide, and frightened, and his thin brown hands were clasped abjectly over his head.

"What in the Seven Seas are you?" Jack said. "You don't look like a dread beastie."

"A stowaway," Barbossa sneered. "Throw him overboard."

"*Lo siento!* I'm sorry! I'm so sorry, señor!" The boy threw his arms around one of Jack's boots and pressed his head to Jack's foot. "I needed help. *No se*—I didn't know what else to do!"

"Well, wrinkling my boots isn't the best way to start," Jack said, stepping back. The boy stayed crouched against the floor of the ship. "Aren't you Spanish?" Jack asked. "You sound awfully Spanish."

"*Si*—yes, I am," the boy said. "I am Diego de Leon. I recently escaped from the fort of *San Augustin*, in Florida."

"A runaway *and* a stowaway," Barbossa spat.

"Sounds like my kind of lad," Jack observed. Barbossa scowled. "You're not related to me, are you?" Jack asked the boy suspiciously.

"No, señor. Please—*por favor*—please help me," Diego said, holding out his hands to Jack. "My friend who escaped with me has been recaptured by the Spanish. I knew only a ship like this could catch them . . . and only a *capitan* like you could lead a successful rescue mission."

"Well," Jack said, stroking his moustache and preening, "that is probably true."

"We're *pirates*," Barbossa reminded him acidly. "Not bleeding-heart-do-gooder-Robin-Hood-hero types. We don't do rescues."

"That is true, too," Jack said with a nod.

"But she needs your help!" Diego pleaded.

"She?" Jack questioned.

"Carolina—she is only fifteen—they were going to marry her off to the governor, a very cruel old man." Diego added a volley of colorful Spanish curses. "She *had* to run away, and I had to help her. Rescuing her from such a fate would be an act worthy of the noble Captain Jack Sparrow."

"Ooooh," Jack said. "The noble Captain Jack Sparrow. I like that." He shook his head. "But my first mate is right, lad. We're pirates, not a rescue party. And we have places to be."

"Yes, about that—" Billy Turner interjected.

"But tell you what," Jack went on quickly, "we'll drop you at the next island, and per'aps someone there can help you, what do you say?"

Diego buried his head in his hands despairingly. "It will be too late," he said. "Carolina will be lost forever."

"Look on the bright side," Jack said, patting the boy's head awkwardly. "Maybe this cruel old governor won't want her anymore, after she ran away like that. Not exactly an auspicious start to the marriage, after all. Maybe they'll just lock her in a nice cell instead."

Diego sighed. "No, her family will make sure the marriage happens. That's what they're carrying all that gold for."

There was a breathless pause as every pirate in the hold perked up his ears.

"Gold?" Jack said casually.

"*Si,*" Diego said without looking up. "Chests and chests of Spanish doubloons, jewels, handcrafted swords—whatever it takes. They are determined to marry her off and get her out of the family's way so she won't be any more trouble to them." He muttered something else in Spanish.

"Hmmm," Jack said, rubbing his chin thoughtfully. "You know, Diego, I believe I've just had a change of heart."

Diego raised his tear-streaked face, looking hopeful.

"Yes," Jack said. "You're right, the noble Captain Jack Sparrow can't just sit idly by and let gold—I mean, this fine young lady—sail off to her doom. Clearly, we must go after the go— I mean, the young lady." He clapped his hands together and rubbed them, grinning. "It's only right and proper. Crew! Trim the jib! Man the helm!

"We've got some rescuing to do!"

CHAPTER FIVE

"**O**h, *captain*, my captain," Billy said sardon-ically as they came on deck.

"Sarcasm is very unbecoming from you," Jack pointed out, striding to the bow. He pulled out his spyglass and studied the ocean ahead.

"I was just wondering," Billy said, "why is it that we are no longer pointed in the direction of North Carolina. As you said we would be?"

"Why, Billy," Jack said in an injured tone, "you heard the lad. There's a damsel in distress who needs our help!"

Billy folded his arms. "Jack, I know perfectly well that we weren't heading for North Carolina even before you found the stowaway."

"Really?" Jack said, keeping his gaze fixed on the horizon. "How odd. Must have words with that first mate of mine. Bit of a loose cannon, he is. It's probably all those feathers on his hat, distracting him. You agree my hat is finer than his, don't you?"

"So you *will* be taking me home after this . . . rescue operation?" Billy asked.

Jack lowered the spyglass and clapped Billy on the shoulder. "Of course!" he said in his usual unconvincing way. Then he strode off to confer with Barbossa.

Billy sighed.

Diego emerged from the hold, blinking in the

bright sunlight. He shaded his eyes and climbed up to where Jack was standing.

"Take a look through here," Jack said, handing him the spyglass. "Tell me if you think that red sail off in the distance might be the one we're looking for."

"*Rojo!*" Diego exclaimed. "Yes, red! It must be!" He peered eagerly through the lens.

"Then never fear!" Jack declared. "We will be upon those Spaniards before the sun sets!"

The sky was dark and starless, full of clouds that hid the full moon.

"I've always said that night attacks are best, really. You know, mate, that ship is going awfully quickly for being laden with as much gold as you say," Jack observed.

"They are rushing home so the wedding will not be delayed," Diego said bitterly. "They cannot wait to be rid of her."

"How shall we do this?" Barbossa said, his eyes glittering with excitement. "Rush in with guns a-blazing, eh? Load the cannons, fire at will? A hand-to-hand-combat free-for-all?"

Jack looked down at his ragtag crew dubiously. Most of them looked sleepy. Their hats were askew and their holsters sagged, and they shuffled in place as if they were wondering when the next barrel of ale would be coming out. Catastrophe Shane was the only one who looked awake, and that was because he'd already been sick with terror twice since he found out they were attacking a ship. His knees shook so hard it seemed they were causing the whole boat to quake. He kept asking for a weapon, but no one wanted to give him one.

Jack shook his head. "Typical Barbossa. Always trying to use blunt force when a little cunning and stealth would do the trick." He turned to Billy. "Tell the crew to douse all the candles and all the lanterns. Not a flicker of light is to be seen. And not a whisper of a sound. Total silence and total darkness."

Billy nodded and hurried off to instruct the crew.

Soon the *Pearl* was plunged into darkness. With her black sails and black hull, she faded into the night like a shadow. She skimmed lightly across the ocean, sneaking closer and closer to the bright Spanish galleon. Soon they could hear carousing and singing, the sound of tankards clanking and voices raised in what sounded, to Jack, rather like gibberish.

"What are they saying?" he whispered to Diego. The boy listened for a moment and then shook his head angrily.

"They are talking about the grand feasting and gorgeous women there will be at the wedding." He listened again. "And now one of them is shouting about how every day will be a grand feast when the Spanish plan succeeds and they control the whole Caribbean."

"Come again?" Jack said sharply.

"And now one of them is shouting about . . ."

"Yes, yes," Jack said, "I've got that part, thank you. But what about this 'plan'?"

Diego shrugged. "I don't know."

"I don't like the sound of that," Jack muttered.

"We're almost upon them, Jack," Billy whispered from below.

"All right," Jack whispered back. "We'll pull alongside and swarm over the rails before they even know we're here. Make sure everyone is armed and ready to go."

"Aye-aye," Billy said.

A moment passed. The Spanish galleon slid closer and closer. Diego could almost smell the ale on the kidnappers' breath. Jack drew his sword and studied its gleaming point. Suddenly a thought struck him.

"Billy!" he called in a loud whisper. "Wait!

When I said 'make sure everyone is armed' I didn't mean—"

BLAM!

All the crew members on both ships threw themselves to the deck and covered their heads with their arms.

BLAM! BLAM!

"Get that pistol away from Catastrophe Shane!" Jack shouted. Billy bravely ran over and tackled the hapless pirate, whose hat—which he had placed back on his head hours after Jack had asked him to remove it—had fallen over his eyes so he was firing wildly into the night sky. Shane thudded to the deck, and the pistol skidded away across the boards.

The Spanish soldiers were all staring in shock at the ship that had appeared mysteriously next to them and then announced itself in such an odd way. But Jack could see that a few of them were already reaching for their swords.

"To arms, men!" Jack yelled. He seized a long hanging rope and ran forward, swinging over to the other ship. For a long moment he hung in the air, the dark ocean yawning endlessly below him, and then he let go of the rope, flew the last few feet, and came crashing down on top of one of the bigger, nastier-looking soldiers, knocking him out cold.

"That was lucky," Jack said, dusting off his hands. "I mean, er, well planned."

"PIRATES!" bellowed one of the Spanish guards.

"Well, obviously," Jack said with a bow and a flourish. "A bit slow on the uptake, aren't we, mate?"

Three of them rushed at him, waving their swords, but he parried their blows with graceful ease. He leaped up onto one of the ale barrels, disarmed one man with a flick of his sword, and casually planted a boot on another's forehead, kicking him to the deck.

Grappling hooks were flying across from the *Pearl* to the galleon as his crew drew the Spanish ship closer and began scrambling across. In the flurry of battle, Diego darted across to Shane's fallen pistol, grabbed it, and hurled himself onto the galleon.

"Carolina!" he cried. "Carolina, *donde estas?*" A Spanish soldier ran at him with his arms outstretched. Diego sidestepped him at the last minute and shoved him overboard. "Carolina!" he called again, rushing to the hatch.

"Ay, Diego," a musical voice said from below. But at first the only person Diego could see coming up the stairs was the scowling, bearded captain who had captured Carolina in Tortuga. Then Diego realized that the captain's hands were tied behind his back and a small, suspiciously attractive pirate was escorting him up the steps with a pistol jabbed into his ribs.

"Not that I don't appreciate the effort,"

Carolina said, smiling at him from under the pirate hat she had stolen in Tortuga, "but this isn't exactly the most subtle way to rescue me."

"At least I'm here, right?" Diego said with a grin. "And I have a ship. What were you going to do, force all the soldiers to take you back to Tortuga with that one pistol?"

"Well, I thought I might also use my charming personality," Carolina said, batting her eyelashes at him.

"How did you get out of your cell?" Diego asked.

"This blackguard here had me brought to his cabin so he could convince me to put on *this*," Carolina said with disgust, holding up a long, frilly, white lace dress in her free hand. "He wanted me to arrive in Florida 'looking like a lady,' he said. I decided to use it to tie him up instead." She pointed to the captain's bound hands, which Diego realized were tied with several strips of Spanish lace.

"Nice work," he said admiringly.

"You know how much I hate dresses," Carolina said. "Especially frilly ones."

Diego dragged the captain onto the deck and fired the pistol into the air. The fighting stopped all over the ship, and everyone turned to look.

"We have your *capitan*!" Diego shouted in Spanish. "We have won the battle! Throw down your weapons!"

Jack jumped off the barrel and sidled over to him. "Is that the captain? Splendid. Tell them we've won the battle and to throw down their weapons."

"Yes, sir," Diego said, exchanging a smile with Carolina. The soldiers were already dropping their swords all over the galleon. Diego raised his voice, and again in Spanish he declared, "Now lead these men to your gold!"

"Oh, and tell them to show us where their gold is," Jack added.

"Yes, sir," Diego said with a straight face. "Now!" he called in Spanish. "You and you and you." He pointed to the three closest soldiers. Gritting their teeth, they led the way down into the hold with Barbossa and a few of Jack's other pirates following right behind.

"Carolina, this is Captain Jack Sparrow. Captain Jack Sparrow, *this* is Carolina." Diego made introductions as Billy took charge of the Spanish captain. Jack saw a girl of about fifteen with long black hair and dark flashing eyes. She was disguised as a boy, in long trousers and a shirt that was too big for her, and there were smudges of dirt on her face, but she was still strikingly pretty. Jack could see right away why Diego had been so intent on saving her from marrying someone else. He also noticed that Carolina didn't seem to recognize the adoring look on the boy's face.

"Thank you for your assistance," she said in

beautifully accented English, holding out her hand regally to Jack. "I would have escaped on my own, but this is certainly more convenient, and I appreciate your gallantry."

Jack made a low bow and kissed her hand. "Well, I am quite a gallant fellow, love," he said. "Never say no to a noble mission. Always . . . doing the right thing, that's me." His gaze slid sideways to the open hatch. Both Carolina and Diego knew he was thinking of his pirates down there with all that gold.

"I'll take Carolina back to the *Pearl*," Diego offered.

"Excellent," Jack said, taking a step toward the hatch. "An excellent—fine—splendid—" He darted down the steps and disappeared into the hold.

"Your *capitan* seems a little odd," Carolina observed. Diego nodded as they wove through the surrendering soldiers to reach the rail, where the two ships were bobbing within easy reach of each other.

"He is odd, but he is brave in his way," Diego said. He hopped up on the rail and reached down for Carolina. She put her small, smooth hand in his, and he felt a jolt of joy in his heart. Only a day earlier he'd thought he'd lost her forever. He put his arm around her to steady her as they stepped across to the *Pearl*'s rail, and then he jumped down and lifted her to the deck of the pirate ship. She put her hands on his shoulders for a minute, and he resisted the urge to wrap his arms around her.

"A pirate ship!" she said with great curiosity, stepping back and looking around. "This is so thrilling. I've always wanted to sail with pirates! Can we stay with them, do you think?"

"I'll show you the captain's cabin," Diego said. "I'm sure Jack will want you to have it."

"No way," Carolina said. "I don't want to be

treated like a princess anymore. I want to be a regular pirate, like everyone else. Maybe they'll teach me to sword fight, Diego! We could learn to sail and battle and plunder just like *they* do! Wouldn't that be wonderful?"

Diego pulled her out of the way as a bag of gold came flying across from the other ship and crashed to the deck where she'd been standing. "Let's try not to get killed by flying loot first," he said with a smile.

Pirates were starting to emerge bearing chests of jewels and gold coins, just as Diego had promised. He led Carolina up to the wheel to keep her out of the way. With great interest she picked up Jack's spyglass, which was leaning against the rail.

"My father would never let me touch these," she said, lifting the glass to peer through it. "He said ladies shouldn't be involved in ships or sailing or anything at all interesting. I'm sure *el*

Cruel would have been the same way." *El Cruel* was their name for the governor she'd been betrothed to. Carolina adjusted the rings of the spyglass for a moment and then sharply drew breath.

"What is it?" Diego asked.

"Do you see it?" Carolina asked, pushing the spyglass toward him. He looked through it in the direction in which she was pointing. For a moment all he could see was the dark mass of clouds reaching down to touch the black sea at the horizon's edge.

Then he felt a shiver of fear as a shape cut through the darkness, an unmistakable outline against the rest of the shadows.

Being Spanish, he and Carolina knew all too well what that shape meant.

"It's the *Centurion*," he breathed. "The Pirate Lord Villanueva is coming."

CHAPTER SIX

"Captain Sparrow!" Diego shouted, leaping down to the deck. "Captain Sparrow! Sir!"

"I like it, I like it," Jack said, popping up from behind a barrel he was rolling down the Spanish ship toward the *Pearl*. "See, Barbossa, that's how everyone should address me. You could learn a thing or two."

"Sir, it's the *Centurion*!" Diego called. "Villanueva is heading straight for us!"

All the pirates turned pale. Several of them

grabbed as much gold as they could hold and hurled themselves over the railings back onto the *Black Pearl.*

"Villanueva! First he steals my crew and now he wants to steal my gold," Jack grumbled. "Bloody pirate."

"Let us stand and fight, gents!" Barbossa said in ringing tones. "Let us defend our prize! Let us show that we are true pirates, brave and bold and—"

"*Or,*" Jack interrupted, "I've got a better idea. Let's run away."

"What?" Barbossa bellowed.

"Why fight when we can outrun them easily?" Jack said. He didn't mention it, but his strange pain, which had faded during the battle, had suddenly returned. He no longer felt energetic and light on his feet. The mossy anchors were back in his chest, weighing him down. The last thing he wanted was another battle, especially with one of the more fearsome Pirate Lords. Besides, they had the loot and the girl—there was nothing to gain, and quite a bit to lose, once Villanueva discovered what lovely piles of gold they had liberated from the galleon.

"All right, men!" Jack cried, waving his sword. "Back to the *Pearl*! And away! Set sail for New Orleans!" The crew began to cast off from the Spanish ship, leaving nothing but tied-up soldiers and an empty hold. Fuming, Barbossa followed Jack onto the ship.

He wasn't the only one who was mad. "New Orleans!" Billy protested. "Why New Orleans? What happened to North Carolina?"

"Yes, yes," Jack said reassuringly. "Not to worry. Just one quick stop on the way! Give the fellows a chance to spend some of this gold while I run a brief errand. Maybe pick up a little more rum while we're there, since we always seem to be out of it for some reason."

"I hope you're planning to dump these two troublemakers there," Barbossa growled, pointing to Diego and Carolina. "We can't even understand half of what they're saying. They could be Spanish spies . . . they could be working for Villanueva himself!"

"We most certainly are not!" Carolina said indignantly.

"That man is a villain and a scoundrel," Diego insisted. "He has no honor—not even the honor among pirates."

"Oh, really? That's rather a dramatic accusation," Jack observed.

"We could tell you something—something that would interest you very much," Carolina said, putting her hands on her hips. "But only if you agree to let us stay with you."

"On the *Pearl*?" Jack said, furrowing his brow. "Don't you have somewhere else to be?"

Diego raised his hands. "Nowhere. We are

fugitives. Where better for us than a pirate ship, where you are always staying one step ahead of the law?"

"True," Jack said, tilting his head. "I am very good at that myself."

"You can't be thinking of agreeing to this," Barbossa spat. "They'll just get underfoot and be in our way."

A few of the other pirates muttered in agreement, exchanging dark glances. They had left the Spanish galleon behind them and were skimming quickly over the waves, keeping the ship dark, and putting as much distance between them and Villanueva as they could.

"We won't be in the way," Carolina said, tossing her head proudly. "We learn quickly. We'll be useful."

"We can help translate," Diego pointed out. "If you capture any Spanish prisoners you want to question—or desire Parlay with Spanish crews—or want to spy on Spanish sailors . . ."

"Hmm," Jack said, stroking his chin. "And you say you have some interesting information for me, darling?"

"*Very* interesting," Carolina said.

Jack knew that Barbossa—and probably most of the rest of his crew—would disapprove, but his curiosity always got the better of him. Besides, nobody said he couldn't change his mind later, once he knew what he wanted to know.

"Very well then," he said. "Welcome aboard!"

Carolina clapped her hands excitedly and hugged Diego.

"Now," Jack went on quickly, before Barbossa could start his bellowing and bellyaching, "what were you going to tell me?"

"It's about Villanueva," Carolina said. "I overheard some of the soldiers talking while they had me locked up. The Pirate Lord is working for the Spanish now. He made a deal with them so he can eventually retire into the Spanish aristocracy. They're planning to take over the whole Caribbean together and then divide it up between them."

"What?" Jack cried.

"What?" Barbossa bellowed.

"That's what I said," Jack pointed out.

"You see?" Diego said. "No honor! He does not even follow the Pirate Code!"

"What do you know of the Pirate Code, boy?" Barbossa snarled. "Your grandfather wasn't even born when captains Morgan and Bartholomew set down the Code for the Second Brethren Court. Some of us have been living by it for our whole lives."

"Not Villanueva, apparently," Diego said.

"If this is true," Billy said seriously, "then it's a good thing we ran. He was coming not just to steal our gold but to free the soldiers . . . and probably sink us, if he could." He shook his head.

"That is their plan," Carolina said. "To sink every pirate ship in the Caribbean and drive out the English and the French forever. The Spanish once controlled these waters completely, and they want to control them again."

Jack set his jaw. "Not while I'm alive," he said. "I am the Pirate Lord of the Caribbean."

"Yes," Barbossa muttered, "and after tonight's dazzling display of courage, I'm sure Villanueva is absolutely terrified."

New Orleans!

The city glittered in the distance as they sailed closer—although not as much, of course, as it had glittered when it was made entirely of silver.

"I'm counting on you, Billy, old chap," Jack said, pulling his friend close. The wind tugged at his long hair, but he knew it wasn't just the wind; it was the strange shadows lurking in the corners of his vision as well. He needed to get rid of them as quickly as possible, before he went truly mad. "It's up to you to keep an eye on the *Pearl* and the crew while they stagger about spending their ill-gotten loot. My advice is to get them as drunk as possible. That should keep 'em busy while Barbossa and I go see Tia Dalma."

"I don't trust that mystic," Billy said. "I don't know why you need to go see her."

"Ah, she's not so bad," Jack said, ruffling Bill's hair. "We go way back. Old friends. I'm sure she'll be delighted to see me. Probably forgotten all about last time. I don't think she's the type to hold a grudge."

"Say, Jack," Barbossa said, joining them at the bow with an apple in his hand. "You know, I could stay with the *Pearl* instead. Wouldn't be

any trouble. Happy to keep an eye on it for you."
He winked and took a large bite of the apple.

"Quite all right," Jack said breezily. "Billy can
handle it. And remember, it's *Captain* Jack." He
tapped Barbossa lightly on the nose and swiped
the apple from him.

Barbossa scowled and stalked away, muttering
something about mangy bilge rats.

The *Black Pearl* sailed grandly into the port,
and Jack remembered his visit to the town long
ago, when he was captain of the *Barnacle*. Now
things were very different. Now he had a whole
crew and a ship to be reckoned with. Not to
mention a quite excellent hat.

He blinked and rubbed his eyes. Was he
seeing things again?

"Jean, mate!" he called down as the *Pearl*
dropped anchor.

A freckled, green-eyed young man with curly
red-brown hair looked up from the line he was

tying to the dock. "Jack!" he cried in delight, smiling broadly.

"*Captain* Jack!" Jack reminded him, waving.

"Of course," Jean Magliore said brightly. "*Captain* Jack." Jean had been one of the first crew members Jack ever had, back when there were just a handful of them sailing the *Barnacle* around the Caribbean. Jack hadn't seen him in years.

Jack didn't even have to offer a place aboard the *Pearl*; Jean was anxious to leave the ship he was working on. "The captain is so boring, Jack," he said as they stood together on the dock, watching the hustle and bustle of ships loading and unloading around them. "You'd barely even know he was there. Not one grand adventure in all the time I've been with him. Not a single ghost or mermaid trying to kill us, not one cursed amulet turning things to bronze. I'm afraid once you've sailed with Captain Jack

Sparrow, nothing else quite measures up. You're sure you have room for me on the *Pearl*?"

Jack beamed. "Absolutely," he said. "Especially now that you don't have that dreadful feline, Constance, following you around anymore. I don't know if I ever mentioned this, but I quite loathed her."

"Oh, you've always made that much perfectly clear, Jack," Jean said. "*Non, mon ami*, my sister is back in human form and having a very normal *human* life, finally."

"*Excellent*," Jack said. "Then you're welcome aboard!"

"But . . ." Jean said nervously.

"No, no, no buts," Jack said, waving his hands.

"I do have one tiny problem," Jean said. "That is, not really a problem, more like a—companion—a duty, kind of—I mean, she has nowhere else to go, so . . . I'm kind of responsible for her."

"Oh, *no*," Jack said, burying his head in his hands.

"She won't be a bother!" Jean assured him. "It's my, uh, *cousin* Marcella, you see. She's been, um, orphaned, and she needs a protector, so that's me, and . . . oh, Jack, say you don't mind. She won't be any trouble at all; she's only a brat to me, really, I'm sure."

"I HEARD THAT."

Jack and Jean whirled around. A skinny girl stood on the dock behind them with her hands on her hips, glaring at Jean. She looked about the same age as Carolina, more elegantly dressed in a long gray gown, but not half so pretty. Jack blinked and rubbed his face. Her eyes looked brown—but then they looked yellow when she turned her head. Yellow eyes? His curse must have been making him see things again.

"Jean!" Marcella said, stamping her foot. "I

am not a brat! I'm not! You must stop saying things like that! It's mean and it's not fair!"

"I'm sorry," Jean said penitently. "Listen, I'm getting us a place on this fine ship here, isn't that splendid?"

Marcella's gaze swept over the *Black Pearl*, from one end to the other. She wrinkled her nose. "It looks like a *pirate* ship," she said disapprovingly. As if the Jolly Roger at the top didn't make that obvious.

"And so it is, love," Jack said. "The fastest, most glorious pirate ship ever to sail the Seven Seas."

The girl gave him the same long, considering gaze she'd given the ship, and her expression of disapproval didn't change. "Hey, wait," she said. "You look like . . . aren't you . . . Jack?"

Jack was startled. Surely he'd never seen this young lady before in his life.

"Er," Jean said quickly. "Give us a moment, Jack." He seized Marcella's arm and drew her away behind a stack of crates, while he talked quickly in French.

Jack gave Diego and Carolina a puzzled look as they came down the gangplank, admiring the busy madness of New Orleans. "No chance one of you speaks French, is there?" Jack asked. They shook their heads. "No, that'd be far too useful. All right, forget it, carry on." He sidled closer to the crates as the Spanish pair walked away, but he couldn't make out anything Jean was saying. He *could* hear Marcella stamping her foot and saying "*NON!*" every now and then, though. That was rather worrisome. Not exactly what he was looking for in a new crew member.

Meanwhile, Barbossa was preparing a longboat to sail up the river. "This is madness, Jack," he said, stacking flasks of fresh water in the boat. "You don't even know where we're going. Just upriver, you've said. What type of direction is that?"

"Never fear, Hector," Jack said expansively. "These things tend to work out in the end."

"Yes, for you and for nobody else," Barbossa muttered.

Jean reemerged, dragging Marcella behind him. "It's all settled," he said happily. "Marcella agrees that this will be a great opportunity for us."

If she did agree, you certainly couldn't tell from the look on her face.

"Er," Jack said, "well then . . . welcome aboard . . . I suppose."

Barbossa scowled at Marcella. "Another woman?" he said. "I suppose our luck can't get much worse."

Marcella turned up her nose at him. "I assure you, dirty man," she said, "that it most certainly can." She marched up the gangplank, her skirts flouncing.

"Oh, dear," Jean said, rubbing his head.

"We'll be off, then," Jack said quickly. "You settle in and take care of . . . all that. We'll be back in two shakes of a feather." He jumped into the boat with Barbossa. "Never understood that phrase myself," he said, settling down in the front of the boat and leaving the seat with the oars for his first mate. "Why would anyone be shaking feathers to tell time? It's quite mysterious." He stared at Barbossa's feathered hat and raised an eyebrow.

Barbossa, realizing that *he* was going to be rowing all the way upriver until they found Tia Dalma, looked as if he was going to say something rather angry. But he narrowed his eyes, held his tongue, and sat down to row. One day things would change. But now was not the time.

The boat set off, weaving between the larger ships until it came to the wide, rushing waters of the Mississippi River. As they moved steadily upstream, Jack studied the banks from below the rim of his hat. His chest was beginning to ache again with the pain and weight of the shadow illness. He needed a cure as soon as possible.

Tia Dalma was his only hope.

CHAPTER SEVEN

Jack started awake and found himself surrounded by darkness. For a moment he could not remember where he was; he felt the bow of a small boat underneath him and the rocking of the water, and he had a strange feeling that his father was sitting nearby, watching him.

Then he remembered the longboat and the river and the trip to see Tia Dalma. His sleep had been haunted by nightmares, dark dream creatures with long arms and slithering bodies pursuing him everywhere, trying to steal the *Pearl* and his freedom and his beloved hat. He sat up and saw Barbossa lighting a lantern. The oars lay still below his hands.

"What's happening?" Jack said. "Where are we?"

"I don't know," Barbossa said, and his voice was more subdued and less sarcastic than Jack had ever heard it. "These are wild and dangerous parts, Jack. I'm not even certain we're on the Mississippi anymore. The boat—it just went where it wanted to. Almost like someone was calling it."

Jack peered into the murky darkness ahead of them. All he could see was the reflection of the lantern in the dark ripples of water right around the boat. From the sound of the waves lapping against land, he guessed that the shores were close on either side of them, but there was nothing to be seen in any direction. Either clouds were covering the night sky, or trees growing close overhead were blocking out the dim sunlight.

Or something much stranger was going on.

An eerie green light flared suddenly ahead and to the left, and the nose of the boat turned toward it. It even sped up a little, like a horse that knew it was returning home.

"Really, boat?" Jack said, scrambling over Barbossa to the rudder. "Head *toward* the strange, creepy light? Is that the best idea?" He tried shoving the rudder from side to side a few times, but the trajectory of the boat stayed the same. Soon they could see that it was aiming for a small tumbledown pier, little more than a collection of boards and rocks sticking out into the river. The green light came from a lantern hung on a pole at the land end of the pier.

The boat bumped gently against the half-rotten wooden planks and stopped.

"Pardon my suspicious mind," Jack said to the boat, "but I'm going to tie you up anyway." He stepped gingerly out onto the pier, which creaked and groaned under him like a pirate whining about swabbing the deck. As the loudest noise in the whispering darkness, it was rather unsettling. No chance of sneaking up on anyone here. Jack lashed the boat's rope to the sturdiest-looking post as Barbossa climbed out and hopped quickly onto land, not trusting the shifting planks of the old pier.

An overgrown path led away from the river through the gnarled trees. Jack left the green lantern where it was and brought the brighter, warmer one from the boat. He led the way forward with Barbossa close behind. The tree branches wound together overhead and feathery vines hung down, brushing against their faces like cobwebs or fingers trying to read their features in the dark.

Finally, after a few minutes of walking, ducking low branches, and stumbling over roots, they came to a small clearing in the trees. Odd, knobbly rocks stuck out of the ground in a strange, even pattern. Jack crouched down to look at one of the rocks. It was old and moss was starting to grow over it, but as he brought the lantern closer he realized that something was carved into the surface of the stone.

He jumped up and leaped back. "It's a grave," he said. "This is a graveyard!" Barbossa took an uneasy step back into the trees. Neither of them wanted to walk on any graves—you never knew how the slumbering spirits below would react.

"Always so clever, witty Jack," Tia Dalma purred in her mesmerizing voice. "It has been too long since I saw you last." The mystic was leaning against one of the trees across the cemetery. Jack wasn't sure if she'd been there all along or if she'd just materialized. She had a way of doing that. She looked simultaneously beautiful and terrifying, as always, and the strange patterns tattooed upon her face almost seemed to dance in the shadows.

Her large, uncanny eyes studied Jack, the flames flickering in their depths more than a reflection of the lantern's light. "A shadow has been laid upon you, Jack."

"*That* part I know," Jack said. "What I *want* to know is how to lay it *off.*"

"Yes," Tia Dalma breathed. She took a step forward, and the silver crab necklace around her neck gleamed in the moonlight. "This is a new enemy you be facing, Jack."

"A new one?" Jack said, outraged. "What'd I ever do to him? Um, her? Him? Do I owe them money? This doesn't have anything to do with that bar wench in Port Royal, does it? Because I had no idea I'd already met her sister. She might have mentioned—"

"Sssssssssssssssssssssssssssss," Tia Dalma hissed, staring into the distance and raising her hands as if she could see something floating in the air. Jack fell silent, squinting to try and see what she saw.

"You be not so familiar with him, but him know you very well," Tia Dalma said. She lowered her voice to an ominous whisper. "Him . . . the Shadow Lord." As she said the last words, the clearing seemed to get darker and a chilly wind swept across the tombstones, trailing skeletal leaves, *whsssh, whsssh, whsssh*. Jack hoped he was only imagining the sound of thunder in the distance. A rainy trip back to New Orleans after a creepy mystical session wasn't exactly how he wanted to spend the night.

"Oh? And what's a Shadow Lord when he's at home?" Jack asked.

"A master of darkness and shadows," Tia Dalma said.

"All right," Jack said, "I probably could have figured that bit out myself. What does he want with me?"

"Him be looking . . . for this," Tia Dalma said. Making a strange gesture, she revealed something small in her hand that glowed a pale, shimmering gold. Jack had no idea what it was, but he knew right away that he wanted it. It was beautiful.

"What is it?" Barbossa asked intently. Jack jumped; he'd forgotten that his first mate was there.

"Shadow Gold," Tia Dalma whispered. "Made by the Shadow Lord." She held it out, and Jack stepped carefully around the graves to get a closer look at it. The object in her hand was a small glass vial with a tiny cork keeping it closed. The golden glow came from the liquid inside. "Him a lord of alchemy," Tia Dalma said, tilting the vial so the liquid slid slowly back and forth. "Him wish to be lord . . . no, *king* . . . of much more."

"Pretty," Jack said casually. "I'd like a better look, though—" He reached for the vial and, quick as a wink, the mystic snapped it into her fist and held it out of his range.

"The Shadow Lord is very angry," she said in a husky voice. "Seven vials of Shadow Gold there be left in the world, and all of dem stolen from him not so long ago." She gave Jack a searching look.

"Wasn't me, love," Jack protested. "For once, I can say it wasn't me. Definitely not. That I can recall. I'm pretty sure. Reasonably sure. More or less . . ."

"I know," Tia Dalma said calmly. "It was I who took dem."

Jack stared at her, openmouthed. "Well, that's not fair, is it? Why's he after me, then? Why isn't it you who's got the nightmares and the tugging and the nasty beastie-thingies slithering about in the shadows?"

"Him not know of me," Tia Dalma said. "Dat be why we meet here, where him cannot see." She indicated the graveyard with her free hand. "And it is not only you he hunts; it is all the Pirate Lords."

"Oh," Jack said, somewhat mollified. "Well, as long as they're all suffering . . ."

"So far, only you," Tia Dalma said. "He is biding him time. Raising him Shadow Army."

"Couldn't him bide him time without cursing me?" Jack objected. He paused. "And please tell me you didn't just say Shadow Army."

"An army that rises from darkness and returns to darkness," Tia Dalma said in a voice like a building storm. "An army that cannot be fought, cannot be stopped, cannot show mercy. An army unlike any ever seen before."

"Well, then," Jack said, "perhaps I'll just pop

back to the *Pearl*, find a quiet corner of the world this Shadow Lord isn't interested in, and stay there until he's quite finished."

"Nowhere is safe," Tia Dalma said, shaking her head. "The Shadow Lord will not rest until all the Seven Seas belong to him—and all the Pirate Lords be dead."

Jack blanched. "Well, that's a bit extreme," he said. "Why's he got such a problem with the Pirate Lords?"

"An old, old hatred," Tia Dalma said. "And only you can stop him, witty Jack."

"Ah," Jack said, backing away, "no, thanks. Lovely offer, but you may have noticed I've been feeling a bit under the weather lately, so, if it's all the same to you—"

Tia Dalma held up the vial of Shadow Gold again. "Here is your cure, witty Jack. Only the Shadow Gold can chase away your darkness." She closed it in her fist again. "But one is not enough. If you want to live, you must find all seven vials of Shadow Gold."

"That should be easy enough," Jack said, "since you're the one who took them, eh?"

Tia Dalma smiled—a smile that was amused and sinister and displeased all at once. "Not exactly I," she said, nodding at something behind Jack.

A horrible scratching noise was coming from the ground near one of the graves. Jack turned slowly to stare at it. He watched as a decomposing hand emerged from beneath the stone cover of a mausoleum. The hand, attached to a similarly decomposing body, pushed the stone aside and brushed dirt and dust from its clothes. Then the body sat up and climbed to its feet and out of the tomb with awful determination.

Barbossa let out a gasp of terror and fled back down the path to the boat.

Jack would have happily done the same, only the new . . . thing . . . was standing between Jack and his escape.

It was shaped like a man, but it looked like no man Jack had ever seen before—and he'd seen some pretty strange fellows in his time. This one swayed slightly from side to side as he shuffled forward. His eyes might have been brown once, but now they were filmy and clouded, staring fixedly into space. Worst of all, bits of skin and flesh seemed to be dropping off him whenever he moved.

"Witty Jack, meet Alex," Tia Dalma said softly. "My zombie."

CHAPTER EIGHT

"**Y**ou've got a zombie?" Jack echoed. "All the rage among mystics these days, are they?'

"Alex, him once sail with the Shadow Lord," Tia Dalma said, ignoring Jack's flippancy. She was watching Alex with a hint of pride. "Him know more about the Shadow Lord than any man alive."

"Well, semi-alive," Jack observed, edging away from the zombie as it shuffled closer.

"So I wakened him," Tia Dalma said, "and

sent him forth to steal me the Shadow Gold. The last vials must be kep' away from the Shadow Lord, else he find more horrible t'ings to do with them."

"And what happened to them?" Jack asked. "Where are they now?"

Tia Dalma frowned at Alex. "Zombies, dey be very obedient, but, I'm afraid, not so clever. I kept one vial, and I tol' him, take the other six vials to the strongest Pirate Lord. I thought the strongest could protect the vials from the Shadow Lord."

Jack searched his pockets, then raised his shoulders quizzically. "He must have gotten lost on the way, because I never received them," he said.

Tia Dalma stared at him and smiled. "Jack be witty, Jack be quick—but Jack be strong? I am t'inking not."

"Hey," Jack said, ruffled. "I am under a curse

here, and am I not still defeating Spanish galleons and finding you in creepy graveyards? You don't see me crawling into a hole and giving up, do you?"

"True," Tia Dalma said with a calculating expression. "Perhaps there be more to witty Jack. But the world will never know unless you find the vials."

"So who'd he give them to, then?" Jack asked indignantly. "Was it Mistress Ching? She scares me a little. Or maybe Sri Sumbhajee, out in India? I doubt it; I hear he has the voice of a four-and-a-half-year-old girl. Oh, tell me it's not Villanueva! That blackguard!"

"No," Tia Dalma said. "Alex, him misunderstand somewhat. Him give the vials to more dan one Pirate Lord."

"Come again?" Jack said worriedly.

"Your compatriots know not what dey have," Tia Dalma said. "I will use de powers of de seas for this, until one Pirate Lord can bring dem all together. Whoever drinks all the vials—every one of dem, Jack—him will be as strong as the Shadow Lord."

"Really," Jack said, interested now. "I like the sound of that."

"If you drink this Shadow Gold, Jack," Tia Dalma said, waving the vial in her hand, "you be healthy again . . . for a time. But you must drink them all if you want to live."

"All right," Jack said impatiently, holding out his hand. "Hand over the shiny lovely, then."

Tia Dalma studied him for another long moment, and then she carefully placed the vial in Jack's outstretched palm. He was surprised at how cold it was. It lay like bottled moonlight in his hand. Was this a wise decision? He didn't really have a choice. With extreme caution, he pried out the cork. Of course he wanted to live. Besides . . . it was pretty.

He tipped back the vial and poured the Shadow Gold down his throat.

As the cold trickle of the alchemical metal spread through his body, he felt himself becoming more alive than he'd ever been before. The weight in his chest melted away, the darkness in his vision vanished, and the air around him was suddenly still instead of plagued by moving shadows. He felt a wild energy surge through him. It was like the first time he stood at the bow of the *Pearl,* captain of his own ship, free as the wind. He felt as if he could run on water, leap off mountains, battle any sea monster.

Yes, he would definitely search for the other vials. He wanted this feeling to last forever.

He blinked and realized that there was another change: he could see in the dark. The forest around the graveyard, previously full of shifting shadows and dangerous unknowns, was now clear as day to him. The gleaming eyes belonged to small night mammals, not ferocious beasts. Nothing was lurking to pop out at him.

Nothing but Alex, of course. But even *he* didn't look so terrifying through Jack's new eyes. Upon closer inspection, the look on his decomposing face was actually a bit goofy.

Not that Jack was getting any closer, of course. The zombie exuded a rather strong smell.

"One question," he said to Tia Dalma. "If you're such an all-fired powerful mystic, why can't you just summon the vials back here right now?" He waggled his hand in the air. "You know—poof and all that?"

"If I could do that," Tia Dalma said, "I'd never have to leave my shack, would I, witty Jack?"

"A nifty power, eh?" Jack mused.

"But not one I possess at the moment," Tia

Dalma said with an ominous glint in her eye.

"All right, so where are these magical, life-saving vials, then?" Jack asked.

"Dat would be tellin'," Tia Dalma responded with a coquettish smile.

"Why, yes, it *would* be telling," Jack said, nodding in agreement. "It would be very *useful* telling. We'd quite like that much telling, instead of all this *not* telling and mysterious gobbledygook, madam."

"I t'ink you have all the knowledge you need, witty Jack," Tia Dalma said. "But I will tell you one t'ing more. There was a vial going to Villanueva, but I stopped Alex in time. This Shadow Gold was sidetracked into safer hands. You might start by looking for it in South America."

"South America?" Jack said. "What, the whole continent? Care to narrow that down for me?"

Tia Dalma shook her head, looking mysterious, as usual. "This might help," she said, reaching into a side pocket and pulling out a handful of knotted string. Jack took it from her and peered at it, holding it at different angles to see if it would turn into something informative. Nope. Still just a bunch of knotted string.

"Wow. String," he said blankly.

"It is a *quipu*," Tia Dalma said.

"Kee-poo," Jack repeated. "Er. Splendid. Always wanted a . . . kee-poo. And is the, er, string going to help?"

"Do you want it or not?" Tia Dalma said fiercely.

"Oh, it's lovely," he said, quickly tucking it into his coat. "Thanks very much."

"And you be taking Alex wit' you," Tia Dalma added, taking the zombie's shoulders and pointing him at Jack. "Follow witty Jack, Alex."

"Hang on," Jack said. "No, don't follow witty

Jack. I don't need a fellow losing bits and pieces of himself all over my ship. For one thing, it's messy, and what's more, bad for morale. Nobody wants the bloke in the next hammock over suddenly dropping his arm on the floor in the middle of the night. Very unsettling."

"Him will be my eyes and ears wit' you," Tia Dalma said. "Him know all there is to know about the Shadow Lord. Also, him was a barber-surgeon, once. Perhaps him could be useful."

Jack raised his eyebrows at the big, rotting hands hanging loosely at the ends of Alex's arms. "No offense, mate, but you're not shaving me!" he said.

"Go now, Jack," Tia Dalma said. "Find the Shadow Gold among your Brethren. Then return, strong, to stop the Shadow Lord and his Shadow Army."

"No problem with part one," Jack said. "I'll get back to you about part two." Despite what

Tia Dalma had told him, he was pretty sure there had to be some part of the world where he could stay out of the Shadow Lord's way. Let someone else stop his "Shadow Army." Jack just wanted to drink the gold and get well. It was a clever plan, really, if he did say so himself.

"Well, thanks for your 'help,' such as it is," Jack said, and then realized that he was talking to empty air. Tia Dalma had vanished. He was alone in the graveyard with only a blankly staring zombie for company.

Jack tilted his head, looking Alex up and down. He waved a hand in front of the zombie's face. No reaction. Not even a blink.

Casually Jack took a big step back, and then back again. Alex shuffled forward two steps.

"Hmm," Jack said. He turned and walked around the edge of the graveyard back to the path. When he glanced over his shoulder, Alex was obediently lumbering along behind him.

Jack sighed. "No chance I can ditch you here, is there, mate?" he asked.

"No chance you can ditch me here, mate," Alex agreed in a monotone.

Jack shrugged. "Think you can remember to call me *Captain* Jack Sparrow?" he tried.

"Think I can remember to call you Captain Jack Sparrow," Alex agreed in the same dull tone.

"Splendid," Jack said happily. At least there was a bright side. "We're going to have to think of a more fearsome pirate name for you, mate. Alex . . . that's a tough one. Angry Alex? Aye-aye Alex. Annoying Alex? Not very piratical, is it?" He sauntered along the trail, testing out names, with Alex close behind him.

As he came closer to the pier, he saw Barbossa crouching by the post, trying to untie Jack's elaborate knots. Luckily, Jack didn't exactly follow the knot-tying rules of most sailors. Or any rules, really. No reason to be predictable, he always said.

"It's all right. Not to worry, mate. I survived," Jack said cheerfully, stumbling up to Barbossa. He reached down and with one quick tug, all of the knots came undone. Barbossa looked angry enough to strangle an alligator. Then he saw Alex shuffling along a few steps behind Jack and he let out a most un-piratelike screech.

"It's—it's right there—" he gibbered.

"Who, him?" Jack said, enjoying the look on Barbossa's face. He pointed over his shoulder at the zombie. "That's just Alex. He's joining the crew. Not so bad, really, once you get to know him. Shame about the smell, though."

Barbossa recovered his poise quickly. "Joining the *crew*?" he snapped. "Well, of course he is. I guess I shouldn't be surprised. If we're a-taking on stowaways and girls now, why not zombies?"

"Why not, indeed?" Jack said, hopping into

the boat. "Alex, I hope you know how to row."

Alex tilted unsteadily as he climbed into the boat, but they managed to avoid a watery debacle. He sat between the oars as Barbossa climbed into the stern, staying well away from the somewhat odorous reanimated corpse.

"I know how to row, Captain Jack Sparrow," Alex said. Jack beamed. Perhaps having a zombie on board wouldn't be so bad after all.

Dawn began to light the edges of the sky as they rowed steadily downriver, and soon they were back in the regular world, surrounded by farmland and fields of tobacco. Jack leaned back with his hands behind his head, basking in the warmth of the Shadow Gold inside him and trying to keep his nose as far away from Alex as possible.

Six more vials of Shadow Gold, and one of them in South America. Perhaps it would be best not to tell his crew the whole story about the Shadow Lord and the army and his illness and all that. No need to worry them, after all. Plus, he wasn't sure how thrilled they would be about embarking on a perilous voyage around the world just to save his life. It didn't seem like so much to ask, considering what grand adventures they would have along the way and what a fine captain he was, but . . . just in case, perhaps he would keep that part of it to himself.

Barbossa wrinkled his nose. "Do you smell that?" he asked.

"Of course I do," Jack said, giving Alex a significant look. "But I was being polite enough not to mention it."

"No, no, not *that*," Barbossa said impatiently. "It smells like smoke—like something's burning."

Jack sat up quickly and examined the boat from end to end. No fire that he could see. But he realized Barbossa was right—there was a burning smell in the air. He stood up and surveyed the fields on either side of the river. They were in a narrow channel skirting around a large island in the middle, so they were fairly close to the reeds and bulrushes swaying along the shore. And off in the distance, Jack could now see several plumes of dark smoke.

"Tobacco plantation on fire," he observed. "Pity. Waste of good tobacco." He cupped one hand around his ear and listened intently. Shouts and rifle shots echoed from across the field. Jack's expression became serious. He could tell that there was a slave revolt underway.

Jack valued freedom above all else and felt strongly about slavery. He'd first parted ways with the East India Trading Company when he'd liberated some of what they saw as cargo and he saw as human beings.

"Look there!" Barbossa said, pointing. "Someone's coming!"

A tall, well-muscled figure was running through the long grass as fast as his legs could carry him. His ebony skin gleamed in the early morning light, and his strong arms swept the reeds aside with a long pitchfork. He had a look of great determination and the speed of a leopard. The crew could hear dogs baying in pursuit behind him.

All at once he spotted Jack standing up in the boat. He changed course instantly, pounding directly toward them. In moments, he had charged through the long reeds and was splashing into the river. Without stopping to ask permission, he gripped the sides of the boat in his powerful hands and hauled himself in. Gasping for breath and dripping with river water, he collapsed onto the boards at the bottom of the boat between Jack and Alex.

Barbossa's lip curled disapprovingly. "Now this is the last straw," he said. "Girls and zombies are one thing, but escaped slaves? Surely you're too sensible to get mixed up in that kind of thing, Jack! Throw him overboard."

Jack sat down, flicking his coat back. "Row, Alex," he commanded firmly. "Row as hard and as fast as you can."

Alex obediently started to row harder and faster, leaning into the oars with all his weight (which resulted in some unfortunate squelching noises). The boat fairly flew through the water, and soon the howls of the hounds and the smoke from the burning tobacco fields were far behind them.

Barbossa was too outraged to speak. He folded his arms and sat glaring, but Jack ignored him.

"Thank you," the fugitive said sincerely to Jack, pressing one hand to his chest as he recovered his breath. His voice was deep and melodious. Water slid down his strong arms and dripped in small puddles on the bottom of the boat. "I do not know how to repay you or show you the extent of my gratitude. You have given me my freedom."

"And by your leave, may I ask what you are planning to do with that freedom?" Jack asked.

"I do not know," the man answered. "My master will search for me. I will have to keep running until I am far enough away to escape him forever."

"Oh, yes?" Jack said. "I happen to know a great vehicle for running far away. It's called a pirate ship."

The stranger's eyes lit up. "You would take me with you?"

Jack offered his hand. "Captain Jack Sparrow," he said. "Know anything about ships or sailing, do you?"

"I can learn fast," the man said. "And my master always said I was a good cook."

Now it was Jack's turn to light up. "Just the thing we need!" he said with delight. "See, Barbossa, this was a lucky break for us, after all."

Barbossa continued to glare at them.

"What's your name, my good man?" Jack asked.

"Gombo," the man replied. "That is what I have always been called, ever since they brought me here. I remember no other name."

"Gombo," Jack echoed. "Well, then, Gombo . . . welcome to the crew of the *Black Pearl*."

CHAPTER NINE

Billy was waiting with the rest of the pirates when Jack and Barbossa arrived back in New Orleans with their two new crew members. The *Pearl* was all ready to go. Catastrophe Shane's hat had been removed permanently, and the pirate had been tied to the mast so he couldn't break anything or accidentally shoot anyone while they set sail. All the pirates were on deck, much happier after a day of carousing in New Orleans.

There was only one small problem.

"Jean," Jack said, beckoning his old friend over as his men worked the giant winch to haul up the anchor. Unlike Barbossa, most of the pirates seemed very appreciative of the addition of Gombo and his strong muscles. They were less thrilled about Alex, of course. Unfair treatment, in Jack's opinion, just because the fellow smelled like rotting meat and lost bits of himself here and there.

Jean came up to Jack, hunching his shoulders and looking sheepish.

"Jean, mate," Jack said, "there seems to be something in *my* cabin."

Jean blushed. "I'm very sorry, Jack," he said. "She won't listen to me. She says a lady shouldn't have to sleep in a hammock with a bunch of pirates."

"Ha!" Carolina said, overhearing. "A lady that delicate shouldn't be sailing with a bunch of pirates in the first place."

"That's what *I* said!" Marcella yelled from behind the closed door to the captain's cabin. "I hate pirates! Dirty, smelly pirates!" She had apparently stacked furniture against the door, so it was impossible to open it. Jack stood with his arms folded. He was very unimpressed by this turn of events.

"Madam, I am the captain!" he called. "And this is the *captain's* cabin, savvy? Where the captain sleeps! And makes decisions! And looks at maps and things! How am I supposed to do any of that if I can't even get through the door?"

"Not my problem!" Marcella called. "We can stay right here in port for all I care!"

Jean tugged on his curls, looking exasperated. "I'm really, *really* sorry, Jack."

"What a baby!" Carolina said loudly. "I haven't done that much whining and crying since before I could walk!"

"I HEARD THAT!" Marcella shouted in outrage.

"You were supposed to!" Carolina shouted back. "You're an embarrassment to women and sailors and pirates and, and . . . and *people* everywhere!"

There was a loud sound of heavy furniture scraping around, and then at long length, Marcella flung open the door of the cabin. Her stringy red-black hair was falling out of its bun, and she was panting with rage. Her strange yellow-brown eyes went straight to Carolina, who stood tall, with her hands on her hips and her long black hair flying loose in the wind.

"How dare you speak to me like that!" Marcella cried. "I am a lady and a Magliore! Not some Spanish peasant girl like you!"

Carolina drew herself up, her eyes flashing.

"Carolina, don't!" Diego warned, but it was too late to stop her.

"Peasant girl! *I* am a Spanish princess,"

Carolina said proudly, "descended from the great kings and queens of Spain, twenty-second in line for the throne. So I think if *I* can manage to sleep in a hammock, so can a mere Creole girl with pretensions to the so-called New World 'aristocracy.'"

Everyone in earshot stared at her, mouths agape. Jack wheeled toward Diego.

"PRINCESS?" he demanded. "Didn't think that was worth mentioning, mate?"

"It doesn't change anything," Diego pleaded. "She still needed rescuing."

"I could have rescued myself," Carolina objected.

"You might have saved us some trouble if you had," Jack pointed out. If New Orleans weren't already fading to a speck behind them, he would have seriously considered going back and leaving her there. But he was on a bit of an urgent mission. Speaking of which . . .

He nipped around behind Marcella and darted into his cabin.

"Mine!" he yelled triumphantly and then closed the door on her startled face.

Evidently Marcella had decided that her first order of business was to redecorate the cabin according to her tastes, which meant rearranging the furniture, dumping all the maps and papers in an untidy pile behind the couch, and redraping the curtains. It also looked like she'd adorned the arms of the upholstered couch with odd scratches. Odd indeed, this one.

With a deep sigh, Jack set to putting things back the way they were. He was nearly finished when there was a knock on the door a few hours later.

"Come in!" he called. "No, wait! Who is it? I'm not here! Go away!"

"Jack," Billy said, poking his head inside. "It's been very nice to see you and Jean again, but I can't help but notice that *this is not the way to North Carolina!*"

Jack squinted out the window, where the setting sun was clearly to their right, proving that they were going south, not north.

"Ah," he said, "yes. Right. We just have to make one more stop. Not to worry, mate! One quick stop and then we'll head right there!"

"Jack," Billy said warningly.

"Tell me something," Jack said, pulling out the *quipu.* "Do you have any idea what this is?"

It worked; Billy was instantly distracted. Unfamiliar things always made him curious.

"Looks like a bunch of knotted string," he said, taking it in his hands. "There could be a pattern to the knots, but I don't know what it means."

"Think it does anything supernatural?" Jack mused. "Tia Dalma gave it to me. So I'm guessing it's a mystical mumbo-jumbo, stringie-wingie thingie."

Billy handed it back quickly. "I don't know," he said, "but speaking of the mystic's, er, *gifts*, I think that zombie might have left one of his fingers in the ratlines of the forward sail. None of the men will go near it."

"Well, tell Alex to go get it himself," Jack said. "He's very obedient, unlike *most* pirates. They could learn a lesson from him."

"He's acting rather odd, actually," Billy said. "He keeps shuffling along the edges of the deck, staring at the land and muttering. I heard him say 'Shadow Army' a few times."

That got Jack's attention. "Hmmm. I'd better go see what's ailing him, then, hadn't I?" he said casually.

Billy was right: Alex was shambling from one end of the rail to the other, staring at the land off to starboard. The other pirates on deck were trying very hard to stay away from him, scrambling to the opposite end of the ship in a giant pack every time he moved.

From the grating over the hatchway came the voice of Marcella. She was stamping around the crew's quarters down below and complaining at the top of her lungs.

"It stinks down here! And it's hot! And stuffy! And what is this hammock made of, canvas? How am I supposed to sleep on that? You better find me a curtain so I can have some privacy, Jean!"

Jean answered in a patient, murmuring voice, but she carried on angrily. Near the main mast, Carolina, looking impatient, shook her head and started to climb the ratlines to the crow's nest. Diego hurried after her.

Somehow the *Black Pearl* had gone from having too few pirates to being overrun with troublemakers. Jack shook his head and approached the wandering zombie.

"Not to interrupt," Jack said blithely, "but

you're going to wear a hole in my deck if you keep this up."

"Coming up on Panama," Alex said, jerking his head at the land, "Captain Jack Sparrow."

Jack couldn't help smiling at that. "Sure we are, mate. What's your problem with Panama? Lovely country. Excellent rum." He wished they could stop, but there was no time for that.

"Not my problem," Alex said, gazing at the horizon. "*His.* The Shadow Lord's." He lowered his voice. "Hates Panama. Did terrible things here. Old grudges. But new victims."

"That doesn't sound very cheerful," Jack admitted. "You're not telling me His Shadowness has already attacked here, are you?"

Alex's eyes stared blankly ahead. "You will see. Soon. Soon you will see."

Up in the crow's nest, Carolina shivered, rubbing her arms. She loved to be up there, above the noise of the ship, just her and the wind and the wild stretches of open sea all around her. But she always forgot how cold it was.

"Here," Diego said, climbing into the basket. He pulled off his coat and draped it around her shoulders, his arms lingering for a moment around her. It was as close as he could get to embracing her.

"Thanks, Diego," Carolina said, putting her arms in the sleeves and buttoning the coat. "If you're sure you don't need it . . . ?"

"I'm all right," Diego said. "I'm used to much worse. Back home in Spain, when I was a boy working in your father's palace, I slept on cold stone floors and worked in the stables through the winter in only a thin jacket." *It was your smile and your eyes and thoughts of you that kept me warm,* he thought but did not say.

"I'm sorry I told them about being a princess," Carolina said. "I know you didn't want me to. Now I will have to work twice as hard to convince them I really want to be a pirate—and that I'm strong enough for it."

"I think that much is obvious," Diego said.

"Really?" Carolina asked hopefully, looking up at him. The basket of the crow's nest was small, so they had to stand close together. Diego could feel his heart pounding. "I'm not like that horrible Marcella girl, right, Diego?" Carolina asked.

"Not at all," he said quickly. "If you want to be a pirate, I know you will be a great one."

"I *do* want to be a pirate," Carolina said, her gaze dropping to the white-topped waves below. It was a gray and windy day, now shifting imperceptibly into dusk. The sea was the color of a gray whale, and bursts of spray flew up against the side of the ship. The mast was swaying more than usual, and Carolina could see that Diego was already feeling a little seasick.

She squinted at the horizon behind them. Suddenly she clutched Diego's arm, and he nearly toppled out of the crow's nest in surprise.

"Diego," she said urgently, "is that a sail? Way over there—do you think it's another ship coming this way?"

He rubbed his eyes and peered into the distance. Carolina was right. There was another ship out there.

"It doesn't mean anything," he reassured her. "It could be going in any direction. It'll probably disappear in a short while."

"What if it's following us?" Carolina whispered, leaning against him with a worried frown. "What if . . . what if it's my family still looking for me?"

"Then we'll fight them off," Diego said, feeling brave enough to touch her face with his fingers. "We won't let them have you. But don't worry yet. It's probably nothing."

She rested her head on his arm, and he took one of her hands in both of his. They watched the sail in the distance for a long, long while. By the time they climbed back down to the deck, they were both sure.

Someone was following the *Pearl.*

CHAPTER TEN

"Nothing to worry about," Jack declared.

Carolina and Diego exchanged glances. "But what if it's the Spanish? What if they're coming for me?" Carolina asked.

"Then we'll give you to them and carry on our merry way," Jack said. Billy kicked him surreptitiously. "I mean, um—that's not going to happen. Nobody can catch the *Black Pearl*, love. It's the fastest ship in the world!"

"That's true," Diego said to Carolina. "This is

the safest place we could possibly be."

"Not when the Shadow Lord finds us," Alex said gloomily.

Diego and Carolina looked at him askance and edged away. Jack tried not to show that he'd been thinking the same thing. He had no idea what kind of ship the Shadow Lord might have. But surely whatever it was couldn't outrun the *Pearl.* Right?

Maybe it was only a pack of Spaniards, or Villanueva. If he just kept moving, there was nothing to fear from them. And they'd stay close to the coast, as they were doing now, so they could make very quick forays for water or anything they needed.

"We'll keep a weather eye on the horizon, just in case," he said.

Marcella stamped up the stairs onto the deck. "EW!" she declared loudly. "Something smells like BURNING! That is SO GROSS! It had better not be dinner! I'm not eating anything burnt! I want fish, and I want it as raw as possible!" She wrinkled her nose. "Somebody get rid of that *horrible* smell right now!"

"What in blazes is she on about?" Jack asked Jean. "I thought we'd all adjusted to Alex by now. No offense, mate," he added to the zombie, who just stared at him blankly.

Jean shrugged, baffled. "Marcella has a remarkably strong sense of smell," he said. "Maybe it's something we just haven't noticed yet."

"Or maybe it's something we *have* noticed, and it's that your cousin is a loony brat," Jack suggested. "Quite frankly, every Magliore I've met thus far, with the notable exception of you, mate, has been a bit . . . well . . . let's just say, are you sure you're not the bait-man's son?"

"Whoever is burning dinner, throw it overboard THIS MINUTE!" Marcella bellowed.

"That is the worst smell I have ever—"

"*I* am the captain on this ship," Jack reminded her, "which is why *I* get the cabin and *I* give the orders around here. Savvy?"

Gombo stuck his head out of the galley, looking offended. "Nobody's burning any dinner!" he said crossly. "I am making the best jambalaya any of you has ever tasted. None of which will be served to anyone who accuses me of ruining food!"

"Jambalaya?" Jean echoed with a dreamy expression.

Diego suddenly lifted his hand to his nose. "Oh," he said. "Captain Jack—I think I'm beginning to smell it, too."

Gombo drew himself up to his enormous full height. "No jambalaya for you, either!" he said ferociously.

"No, no," Diego said. "It's not your cooking, I'm sure of it. It's something farther away." He

143

pointed to the land off to starboard. "Something over there, I'm guessing."

Alex let out a low moan and pressed his hands to his face with an unpleasant squishing sound. "The Shadow Army," he groaned. "The Shadow Army has been here."

The rest of the pirates fell silent as the strange smell reached all their noses. It was as Marcella had described it: a charred, sickly, smoky smell that permeated their lungs instantly. They all felt as if they would never be free of it again.

Then they saw the ruins.

The fort's tall, thick walls now lay in scattered piles of stone, as if giants had kicked them in, then brutally crushed the rest of the town beneath their feet. Blackened shells of houses were visible inside the town, where fire and the Shadow Army had ravaged every inch and left nothing alive. Worst of all, along the beach lay strange, bloodstained lumps that nobody recognized as corpses until Carolina let out a small gasp, covering her mouth.

Diego moved instantly to block her view, but she stepped back and nodded at Marcella. "Too late. Don't let her see," she whispered.

Obediently, Diego went over and took Marcella's arm, steering her away from the horrifying sight. Jean's cousin looked too over-whelmed to understand what she was looking at. She let Diego lead her to the port side, where there was nothing to see but the comfortingly empty sea. Diego offered her his handkerchief, and she pressed it to her face, taking shallow breaths.

"Something evil happened here," Gombo said in his deep, solemn voice. "I have seen many evil things, but this . . . it reeks of the Other World."

"I think you might be right about that," Jack said.

"The Shadow Army," Alex moaned again, refusing to look. "The Shadow Lord. He did enough evil here, long ago, with his army of men. But this is much worse, so much worse."

Even Barbossa had nothing sarcastic to say. He pulled his hat down further and turned the wheel, taking them far away from the scene of devastation and death as fast as they could sail. The rest of the pirates returned silently to their chores. Their captain stood alone, contemplating the handiwork of his new enemy.

Something tugged at Jack's coat.

He jumped, turning quickly to see nothing but shadows disappearing into more shadows along the length of the deck as night descended on them. Once again, he felt a cold weight stealing into his chest. The Shadow Gold was wearing off already, or perhaps being near the Shadow Army's aftereffects sucked away some of the gold's power.

He needed to find the second vial. And fast.

"**A**ll right, men," Jack said. "And, uh, you," he added to Carolina. He dropped the *quipu* on the large round table in his cabin. It was the next morning, and the sun shone brightly through his windows, but it couldn't chase away the nightmares that had plagued him all night. It was time to get to the bottom of things. "What is this wretched thingie and what does it do?"

Diego, Carolina, Billy, and Barbossa all leaned in to study it. The knotted string lay on the table in an innocent, unreadable tangle. Carolina reached out and poked it. Like any string, it did not react.

"Looks like string, sir," she said with a straight face. "With knots in it."

"Thank you for your *brilliant observations,*"

Jack said. "What does it *do*, and how will it help me find the Shadow Gold?"

Diego picked it up and rubbed the knots between his finger and thumb. "Maybe you have to do something to it," he suggested. "Like get it wet?"

Jack picked up a pitcher from the table and promptly poured water all over the *quipu*. Upon reflection, he realized he probably should have moved the maps and everything first. Billy and Diego scrambled to mop up and save the parchments as Jack lifted the *quipu* again and squinted at it.

"Ah, yes," he said knowingly. "Now it looks like *wet* string." He gave Carolina a sardonic look. "With knots in it."

"Perhaps you have to wear it," Carolina offered.

"Or eat it," Barbossa said. "Or, I know, use it to strangle yourself with." The others looked at

148

him, and he made an innocent face. "What? I thought we were brainstorming."

Jack took off his beloved hat and gingerly put the *quipu* on his head, on top of the red bandanna he always wore. Water dripped down into his ears. And judging from the way Diego and Carolina were smothering giggles, he looked perfectly ridiculous.

"You must be supernatural," he said to the *quipu*, taking it off and shaking it in his hand. "Why would a mystic give me a bunch of string? Not that Tia Dalma is always the most lucid dame, but surely it has to do *something*."

A piercing shriek came from the other side of the cabin door, followed by a few loud crashes, some shouts, and finally, an ominous splash.

Jack looked at Barbossa. Barbossa looked at Jack. They both looked at Billy.

"I'll just go check on that," Billy said. But before he got to the door, it opened. Jean leaped in and slammed it shut behind him.

"Nothing. Don't worry," he said quickly, pressing his back to the door. "It's all under control."

"Let me guess," Jack said, pressing his hands together and pointing them at Jean. "Our darling Marcella has had another tantrum."

Jean winced. "Gombo asked her to swab the deck. He said she could at least contribute to things around here if she was going to eat so much of the food he cooks."

Carolina hid a grin. "Unfortunate phrasing," she pointed out.

"You have no idea," Jean said. "So there was a bit of a quarrel, but it's all right now."

Jack sat up straight. "She didn't throw Gombo overboard, did she?" he asked. "I won't be pleased if she did. We'd only turn around for a cook that good and my hat!" Seeing Billy's expression, he added, "Oh, and for you, too, mate. Absolutely." He winked at Barbossa, who only frowned in reply.

"No, no," Jean said. "Not Gombo. Only . . . the swabbing mop and bucket."

"Hmm," Jack said. "Delightful."

"Hey," Jean said, suddenly spotting what they'd been looking at. "What are you doing with a *quipu*?" He walked over to the table and picked up the discarded string. "And why is it all wet?"

"Never mind that," Jack said. "You know what this is?"

"Of course," Jean said. "It's for sending messages. The pattern of knots spells out the message, so it can be carried back and forth without being read, because only a few people know how. I heard the Mayans talking about them when I was in Tumen's village.* Of

---

* Tumen is another sailor who was part of the *Barnacle*'s crew.

course, the Mayans think their alphabet is far superior."

"Superior to what?" Jack asked.

"Don't you know?" Jean said. "The people who use *quipus*. The Incas."

"Ah, yes," Jack said, furrowing his brow and looking knowledgeable. "The Incas."

"Who are the Incas?" Billy asked.

"Oh, come now. Everybody knows the Incas, mate," Jack said. "Go on, Jean, tell him."

"They live in the mountains of South America," Jean said. "They used to be very powerful, before the Spanish came."

Jack nodded sagely. "Obviously. Well, that clears things up." He stood up, grinning. "The Incas have my Shadow Gold. And I'm going to get it back!"

CHAPTER ELEVEN

The *Black Pearl* sailed along the dark green coast of South America as Jack held up his map and tried to figure out where they were. Up in the crow's nest, Diego and Carolina searched with the spyglass for the ship that had been following them, but it looked like they'd managed to lose it.

"Regular maps," Jack muttered, squinting at the charts. "Very confusing. A cartographic conspiracy, say I. Give me a treasure map any day."

"The Incas live here, in the Andes, mostly in Peru," Jean said, leaning over his shoulder, turning the map right side up, and tapping a section of the continent.

"Well, how are we supposed to get there?" Jack asked, turning the map upside down again. "By sailing all the way to the bottom and up the other side? That's absurd." He peered at the thin shape of Panama. "You know, somebody should build a canal here," he said, pointing at it. "That would speed things up nicely."

Barbossa snorted. "Oh, yes. I'm sure someone will get right on that," he said.

"I guess we could leave the ship up north and get there over land," Jean said dubiously.

"Capital!" Jack said. "Let's do that! Barbossa, find a place to hide the ship."

Grumbling, Barbossa swung the ship closer to shore. Soon they found an inlet that led to a sheltered cove, surrounded by swaying palm trees and thick jungle. White sandy beaches curved around them in a welcoming crescent of warm sand. It was easy to sail the ship right up into the shallow water. Jack's crew jumped out and began to haul the *Pearl* up on the sand.

"All right," Jack said, surveying his options with a doubtful expression. "Barbossa, Diego, Gombo, Jean, you're with me. Billy, you stay and guard the ship with the others."

"What about me?" Carolina said. "I want to help."

"And *I* don't want to be left alone with a bunch of *smelly pirates,*" Marcella said, stamping her foot. She sidled over and wrapped herself around Diego's arm. "I want to go with Diego."

Diego was more than a little alarmed by this turn of events. Why, oh, why couldn't it be Carolina who couldn't bear to be parted from him?

"No, no, no, absolutely not," Jack said.

Marcella looked furious, took a deep breath, and opened her mouth to scream. "All right, shut it," Jack said quickly. "Fine. Just don't blame me if you both get eaten by panthers."

Marcella opened and closed her mouth several times, but didn't seem to have anything to say to this.

Carolina just smiled.

They climbed over the rail and splashed through the water up to the beach. Diego edged away from Marcella and studied the sand curiously. He walked up the beach to the high tide mark as the others caught up.

"What is it, Diego?" Carolina asked.

"Yes, what is it, Diego?" Marcella said instantly, crowding Carolina aside.

Diego held out his hand, keeping her back. "Wait, don't walk here yet," he said. "Captain Sparrow, come look. I think someone has been here before us." He pointed to some indentations in the sand. "The tide has nearly washed them away, but I think there were footprints here, coming up the beach. Meaning another ship—and whoever it was must have gone into the jungle." He glanced around. "Maybe over there; it looks like there could be a path."

"If they're not Incas, I'm not interested," Jack said. He glanced around at the thick mass of foliage pressing in around the beach. "Well, perhaps a path would be useful."

It was, in fact, a path, although it looked like it was meant to be hidden from the beach by a screen of woven palm fronds. When they pushed through, they could see signs that someone— more likely several people—had come through with machetes or something similar and carved a definite route through the undergrowth.

"I don't like this," Gombo said darkly. "It might be of the Other World. Where could it lead? Would we want to meet whoever might be at the end of it? No, I fear we have more enemies than friends out there. I say we stay away from the path."

"That's stupid!" Marcella objected. "It's so much easier to take the path. We'll never get anywhere climbing through all this leafy stuff!"

"And surely whoever was here has gone," Diego said, "since there is no boat in the cove waiting for them."

"Thank you for agreeing with me, Diego," Marcella said, batting her eyelashes at him.

Carolina hid a smile as Diego turned red.

"I take your point, Gombo, mate," Jack said, "but I'm afraid that we are in rather a hurry, so the fastest route is, ipso facto, ergo sum, *e pluribus* something or other, the best route. And maybe it leads to the Incas." He took out the *quipu* and shook it. Nothing. Ah, well. He put it back in his pocket and set out down the path, drawing his sword in case they did run into any nasties.

Gombo offered to scout ahead, and they all watched him silently run off along the path on bare feet.

"How are you feeling, Jack?" Barbossa asked solicitously. "Ill? Slightly unwell? Horribly unwell? Close to death? How close to death?"

"I'm quite all right," Jack insisted, trying not to jump every time he saw a shadow moving beside him.

It was odd to be on land again after days on the ship; the ground seemed to wobble below them, and the sounds of the jungle were very different from the sounds of the sea. Instead of rushing waves and seagulls, their ears were full of the noise of parrots squawking, monkeys howling, and insects chirping and buzzing all around them.

Carolina liked the feeling of having "sea legs,"

as if she really belonged on a ship instead of on land. But she was also excited to be exploring a whole new place. No one in her family had ever been anywhere like this before! She laughed quietly.

"What?" Diego asked, amused.

"I was just picturing my aunt's face if she could see me now," Carolina said, imitating the old woman's pinched, disapproving expression. Diego chuckled.

"I don't see what's so funny about getting eaten alive by mosquitoes and dragging my pretty dress through all this mud," Marcella butted in.

"Actually, I bet Aunt Reynalda's face would look a little like that," Carolina whispered to Diego, and he laughed out loud. Marcella narrowed her eyes at Carolina, but the Spanish princess was too busy gazing up into the trees to notice.

Gombo came padding back down the trail, holding one finger to his mouth to indicate silence. "There's a fort up ahead," he whispered.

"A fort?" Jack echoed. "Here? What kind of fort?" All of them remembered the last fort they had seen, in the town devastated by the Shadow Army.

"It flies the Spanish flag," Gombo said.

Jack sighed theatrically. "What are they all doing here?"

"And more important," Gombo pointed out, "why don't they want anyone to know they are here? Why has the fort been so carefully hidden?"

"Did you see many guards?" Barbossa asked. "Is it well fortified?"

"Irrelevant," Jack said, waving his hands. "We'll just sneak past and head straight on into the mountains."

"But think about it, Jack," Barbossa argued.

161

"They probably have something to hide. Something worth *stealing*."

"We don't have time for crazy side excursions based on wild theories," Jack said. "Not unless they're *my* wild theories."

"What if I checked it out myself?" Barbossa offered. "You go on ahead, and I'll meet you back at the ship."

Jack was too preoccupied with his illness and his quest for Shadow Gold to notice the ominous gleam in Barbossa's eyes. "Very well," he said. "Do what you like. I can find the Incas without you."

But Barbossa's sinister machinations had not escaped everyone's notice. "I'll go with Barbossa," Diego offered. He didn't trust the first mate out of Jack's sight. He had a feeling that Barbossa would be more than happy to sail off with the *Black Pearl* as soon as he got a chance.

"I, too, will go with Barbossa," Gombo said, for the same reason. He did not necessarily believe Jack was the best captain—too much jumping at shadows, for one thing—but he owed Jack his loyalty for helping him escape, and he was quite sure Barbossa would be a far worse captain. No, he intended to keep an eye on Barbossa for Jack, even if Jack did not know it.

"No need for that," Barbossa said with a sly smile. "I can manage alone."

"It's all the same by me who goes where," Jack said. "But hurry up and decide—I have Incas to find, Shadow Gold to acquire, and a Shadow Army to hide from. . . ."

"We're going with you," Gombo said firmly to Barbossa.

"Fine." Barbossa spat. They had crept forward to the point where they could see the tall stone walls of the fort ahead of them. The path wound past it and continued uphill toward a mountain peak in the distance.

"I want to go with Diego," Marcella piped up.

"A capital plan," Jack said. "Much better idea than coming with me. You go ahead with good old Diego." He pushed her in Diego's direction.

"Absolutely not," Barbossa said. "I'm not risking my neck dragging a girl into a Spanish fort with me. Especially *this* girl."

"Shouldn't you stay with me, cousin?" Jean asked.

"I *want* to go with *Diego*!" Marcella insisted, stamping her foot. "He's the *only* one who *understands me*!"

"I am?" Diego said, surprised. "I do?"

"Alas, the dire consequences of lending a girl your handkerchief," Carolina whispered to him, her eyes sparkling with amusement.

"All right, that's settled, then," Jack said, waving his hands. "She goes with you. Captain's final word. Farewell, good luck, have fun storming the fort and all that." He scampered ahead on the path, and Jean and Carolina followed him quickly. Carolina glanced back once, meeting Diego's gaze, and mouthed "good luck" to him with a little wave.

I think I'm going to need it, Diego thought as Marcella, with a triumphant smile, wound her arm through his.

"It is possible this was not the best plan," Jack admitted after an hour of climbing through dense jungle. He paused to examine the tree in front of him, which looked much like the tree behind him, and the tree beyond that, and every other blasted tree he'd seen since the beach. The path had ended shortly beyond the fort, and now he and Jean and Carolina were all covered in dirt and insect bites and scratches from all the branches that kept whipping back in their faces.

The trees were finally beginning to give way to more open terrain, but the air was also getting colder as they climbed farther and farther up the hillside.

"What plan?" Carolina asked. "Pick a continent and just start walking? Figuring you'll run into someone who lives there eventually? What could be wrong with that plan?"

Jack squinted at her. "I think I liked you better when you were more worried about me throwing you off my ship."

"Let's look at the *quipu* again," Jean suggested. "Maybe we're missing something."

Jack took it out and walked ahead, aiming for a patch of sunlight where the tree cover was thin over a rocky slope. "Useless bunch of string," he muttered. "Useless pile of kno— AAAAAAAAAAAAAAAAAAAAAAAAAAA!"

Jack vanished into the earth with a startled yell.

166

"Jack!" Jean shouted, sprinting forward with Carolina. "Jack, are you all right?"

"Of course I am." Jack's voice came from down below. He had fallen into a slanting tunnel in the side of the hill, and now he looked up at them, tilting back his hat. "Never better. Did that on purpose, obviously. This is just what I was looking for." He spread his arms, indicating the cave around him.

"A hole in the ground?" Carolina asked.

"A network of secret tunnels," Jack said with emphasis, pointing to the darkness behind him. "Come down and see."

"But how do you know it's any help?" Jean asked.

"Shouldn't we pull you out instead?" Carolina asked.

"One, always follow secret tunnels," Jack answered. "That's just obvious. You'll learn when you've had a few more supernatural adventures. And B, look at *this*." He held up the *quipu*. It was now glowing with an eerie silver light in the darkness of the cave. Jack smiled. "Told you it was mystical!"

Carolina and Jean carefully climbed down to join him. Tunnels extended from the cave in all directions, but as Jack demonstrated, the *quipu* glowed brightest when he chose the tunnel to the left, so they decided to follow that.

"*Incroyable,*" Carolina whispered, touching the glowing *quipu*. "How does it do that?"

"Supernatural whatsits," Jack said offhandedly. "You get used to it after a while."

"Especially if you hang around Jack for very long," Jean pointed out.

"Ahem . . . *Captain* Jack," Jack said.

They walked and walked for a long time, staying close together to share the small circle of light cast by the *quipu*. Each time the tunnels branched, they watched the glowing string to decide which path to choose. The stone walls on either side of them were cold and damp, and they could hear water dripping in the caves they passed and underground rivers rushing down faraway tunnels. Otherwise it was very still, especially after the wild chatter of the jungle, and Jack became more and more aware of the darting shadows that only he could see.

But finally the tunnel began to slant up and up and up, and then they could see light ahead of them. With a happy cry of triumph, Jack sped up, leading the way out of the tunnel into a wide-open space.

It was sunrise, which didn't make sense—it had been the middle of the day when they went into the tunnels, and they couldn't have been down there *that* long. Even more impossibly, they were now very clearly standing on a mountaintop surrounded by other mountains, a long, long way from the sea. Jack looked down at the *quipu* in puzzlement. "Did you do that?" he asked it.

"Jack," Jean said warningly. Jack turned around and realized that scattered across the mountaintop was a small city with stone temples, stairs, and wells built high above the jungle. And this city was most definitely occupied. A crowd was gathered around an altar, where a man in a long robe stood holding a tall, golden spear. He was glaring at Jack. In fact, they were all glaring at Jack.

"Oh, bugger," Jack said.

He had found the Incas . . . but the Incas were clearly not very pleased about it.

Chapter Twelve

The fort was small, but the solid stone walls were thick and steep, and the noses of small cannons poked over them ominously. Double wooden doors at the front were reinforced with an iron portcullis. Up above, the Spanish flag fluttered in the warm breeze. But there were no signs of guards—no signs of any human life at all.

"Maybe there's nobody here," Gombo said. "Perhaps they left their loot unguarded, thinking the jungle was enough to guard it for them."

Diego shook his head. "I know the Spanish army," he said. "The generals would never take that risk. They will have left a squadron here to keep an eye on the fort, no matter what's in there."

"Wow," Marcella said, leaning on his arm and batting her eyelashes. "You're so smart, Diego. Not like some people." She shot Gombo a glare and he glared back. The fight over swabbing the deck had never quite ended between the two of them.

Diego nodded at the flag above. "But I also know Spanish soldiers, and most would happily take any chance to be lazy. They are probably all inside having an afternoon siesta, or gambling, or just sitting around complaining about what a boring place they are stuck in."

"That's not just Spanish soldiers," Gombo said. "That's almost every man I've ever met, except perhaps this Jack Sparrow."

Barbossa grunted. "Well, let's make things a little *less* boring for them, shall we?" he proposed with a cunning grin.

"First we need to find a way in," Gombo said, carefully studying the walls.

"Oh, I can't *wait* to hear your clever plan," Marcella sniped. "Let me guess—march up to the door and knock?"

Gombo turned and looked at her slowly. A grin spread across his face. "Why, Miss High-and-Mighty," he said, "I believe that just might work."

The other two turned to look at her as well.

"Oh, no. No, no, no, no," Marcella said. "Absolutely not! No way! Are you insane? Me? I won't! I won't do it! You can't make me!"

Fernando Ruiz could not wait to be sent home to Spain. He dreamed of the long paved streets of Madrid, the fiery eyes of the flamenco dancers, the drama and glory of the bullfights. He had thought to capture that glory by becoming a soldier in the Spanish army—but instead here he was, stuck in what was basically a stone prison in the middle of a jungle, without a *taberna* or a bullfight or a flamenco dancer for hundreds of miles in any direction. Nothing but heat and buzzing insects persecuting him day and night. His red-and-gold uniform made his skin itch, and his tall leather boots made his feet sweat and smell horrible.

The other three men at the table looked equally hot and lifeless. Even the cards in their hands were limp and damp with sweat. The captain waved away a fly and then paused with his hand still in the air. All four of them raised their heads and listened.

"Was that knocking?" asked Bartana, one of the card players. "I could almost swear I heard knocking."

"And shouting . . . maybe?" mused Salamanco, another soldier.

"Out here in the jungle?" Ruiz scoffed. "Who could it be?"

"Villanueva?" Salamanco guessed placidly. He dropped a card on the table, and the captain scooped it up.

"A day early?" Bartana said, scratching his nose. "That doesn't seem like him. No matter how excited he is about the gold we're holding for him."

"Well, who else in this godforsaken wilderness knows we're here?" Ruiz challenged.

"The ones looking for that princess," the captain pointed out, laying down a card. "We got word to keep an eye out for her. They have no idea where she's vanished to."

"Yeah," said Fernando, "I'm *sure* there's a princess knocking at the gate right now."

"I guess you better go find out," the captain said, nodding at Ruiz.

"Why me?" Fernando protested. "Why not one of them?" He jerked his thumb at the other two soldiers, who were of equally low rank.

"Because you lost the last round," the captain said calmly, "and because you're the only one who's going to bother anyway."

Cursing roundly, Fernando shoved his chair back from the table, slapped his cards down, and stormed out into the courtyard. The knocking at the gate sounded less like knocking now and more like someone throwing big rocks at the doors.

He slid open the eyehole and peered out. His jaw dropped in shock.

An angry girl stood outside the gate, her hands on her hips, scowling. She saw his eyes appear in the slot, and her face lit up.

He quickly slammed the slot shut again. Was he seeing things? Had five months in the jungle finally driven him mad? Or . . . was it possible that an escaped Spanish princess really was standing right outside the gate of his fort, knocking? She didn't look Spanish, but you couldn't always tell. His mind instantly filled with thoughts of the giant reward that had been offered. And while she was waiting for the ship to take her home . . . perhaps he could teach her to flamenco dance.

He slid open the slot and discovered that the girl's face was still on the other side. Startled, he jumped back, and she stuck her tongue out at him. He rethought his flamenco dancing idea. Just the reward would be sufficient.

"Who are you?" he demanded.

"Jibber jabber jibber," she said, or, at least, that's what it sounded like to him. He guessed she was speaking French.

"Are you not the Spanish princess?" he asked, disappointed. Surely if she were, she'd be speaking Spanish, like him.

"Jibber jabber!" she yelled. "Blah-blah-blah!" She smacked the door and stamped her foot. He didn't need to speak French to figure out that she was demanding to be let inside.

Well, what harm could that do? Perhaps one of the other soldiers could figure out what she was saying. And it wasn't as if one lost girl could be any threat to the fort. He signaled to her to wait, and then he went to the mechanism that opened the gate. With loud creaks and groans, the portcullis went up and the doors swung open.

Marcella marched inside, looking pleased with herself and very haughty. Although her bedraggled gown did not match her regal demeanor, Fernando found himself bowing gallantly anyway.

He straightened up to find a pistol in his face.

"Surprise," Barbossa said with a wolfish smile. "Thanks ever so much for inviting us in." He clubbed the soldier over the head, and Fernando passed out on the yard's cobblestones.

Behind Barbossa, Gombo frowned. "Let's try to do this with minimum bloodshed," he said. "We don't need the Spanish government any angrier at the *Pearl* than it already is."

"Stupid princess," Marcella said, tossing her head. "I wish we could get rid of her and just keep Diego."

"Speaking of Diego, where is he?" Gombo said, glancing around. "He should have been inside by now—we watched him scale the wall at the back."

"Oh, I hope he's all right!" Marcella said, clasping her hands. "I couldn't believe how bravely he climbed those steep stones, using only a few edges for footholds! I so hope nothing terrible has happened to him!"

Gombo rolled his eyes. "It is not such an amazing trick, climbing a stone wall," he said gruffly.

"Well, I didn't see *you* volunteering," Marcella snapped.

"*I* don't speak Spanish," Gombo reminded her. "*I* could not gather information the way he could by eavesdropping before we got in."

"Exactly," Marcella said. "Just one reason why he's a hero and you're not." They glowered at each other.

"I'm here," Diego said, appearing in the low doorway of the inner building of the fort. He had a sword pointed at a Spanish soldier, who was gaping at the four intruders in astonishment. "His friends are tied up in there." Diego nodded behind him. "And this gentleman has kindly agreed to show us to the office where they are storing the gold for Villanueva."

Barbossa's eyebrows arched. "Villanueva?" he said. "There's gold for him here?"

"So I overheard," Diego said. "A whole chest of it. His deal with the Spanish must be going well." He nudged the soldier with his sword. "Take us to the gold," he said in Spanish.

The soldier nodded, blinking, and led the way inside. Marcella flounced ahead of Gombo, and Barbossa brought up the rear, training his pistol in all directions. But the fort was quiet. They met only two other soldiers on the way to the office, and those were easily taken care of by tying them up and stuffing them into a closet. It seemed that Diego was right—most of them were peacefully enjoying their afternoon naps.

"Here," the soldier stammered to Diego in Spanish, stopping at one of the doors. "This is the commander's office. He has sailed out to meet Villanueva and bring him back here. They should return tomorrow."

"*Gracias,*" Diego said to him. "And in exchange for your help, I will help you as well." He leaned toward the soldier and whispered, "I have heard a rumor about that Spanish princess everyone is looking for."

"*Princessa Carolina?*" the soldier said eagerly. Marcella caught the name Carolina and looked up with a scowl.

"Yes," Diego said, still in Spanish. "I have heard that she took passage on a ship bound for Ireland. It left two days ago, but it was supposed to stop in New York, Boston, Maine, Canada, and Greenland along the way. If they want to find her, they should start by looking in all those places."

The soldier nodded, repeating the cities as he tried to memorize them. "*Nueva York*, Boston," he said, "yes, yes, thank you, good sir. They will reward me well for this information!" His face fell. "That is, after they punish us for allowing the fort to be robbed in the first place."

Diego felt a twinge of guilt, but it was worth it to throw Carolina's family off her trail. "Sorry, my friend," he said. Gombo took the soldier aside, tied him up, and sat him gently down on the floor of another closet to await rescue.

As they opened the door to the commander's office, Gombo tilted his head at Diego. "I didn't understand most of what you said to the man," he said, "but you did something clever, didn't you?"

"I hope so," Diego said fervently. "I would do anything to protect Carolina." He didn't notice Marcella's face darken angrily.

The office was small and square with only one window high up in the wall. There was a heavy oak desk, a pair of plain cabinets, a map of the Caribbean hanging on the wall, and one very large chest which looked very promising.

Barbossa pushed past them and hurried to the chest. It wasn't even locked—they really must have thought no one would find the fort out in the jungle. He flung open the top, and the crew was downright awed at the sight of the gleaming pile of coins inside. The whole room seemed to be lit up by them. Gombo peeked out into the passageway and closed the door.

"Quickly now," Barbossa said. "Let's seize the gold and get out of here." He chuckled, rubbing his hands together. "I wouldn't like to be this commander when Villanueva arrives and finds he is not getting paid for his deceitful, black-hearted schemes."

"I don't know why you're so outraged by that," Marcella said, plopping herself on the edge of the desk and swinging her feet. "I mean, he's a *pirate*. Of *course* he's deceitful and black-hearted. What did you expect? You're all like that, aren't you?"

Barbossa drew himself up with proud fury. "Most certainly not," he said. "Deceitful and black-hearted, perhaps we are. But we would never go against the Code. Well, perhaps for good reasons. But mostly never."

"What code?" Marcella asked. Rummaging in one of the cabinets, Gombo found a couple of canvas sacks. He passed one to Diego, and they began to fill them with gold coins as Barbossa strode from one end of the office to the other, explaining intently.

"The Code was set down by the Brethren Court many many years ago," Barbossa said.

"What's a Brethren Court?" Marcella interrupted. She spotted a bowl of candy on the commander's desk and seized it, stuffing some into her mouth.

Barbossa took a deep breath, his nostrils flaring. "The Brethren Court is composed of the nine Pirate Lords, the greatest pirates in all the Seven Seas," he said, then paused. "And also Jack."

"Jack's a Pirate Lord?" Marcella mumbled around a mouthful of candy.

"Somehow," Barbossa muttered darkly. "Most

likely through some typical Jack trickery—or luck, he has an uncommon amount of that, too. We'll see how long that lasts."

Diego and Gombo exchanged glances, but the first mate didn't notice.

"At any rate," Barbossa went on, "the second Brethren Court drew up the Pirate Code. Two of the Pirate Lords, Morgan and Bartholomew, figured it out and wrote it down, and that's what we've all lived by ever since." He shook his head. "I don't know what the world is coming to, pirates siding with the army against other pirates. Have they no honor? Have they no pride? Can't they just steal our treasure and raid our ships without kowtowing to Spanish commanders as they do it? It isn't right, I say."

Marcella shrugged. "Still sounds all the same to me."

Barbossa seemed to realize who he was speaking to. "Lasses, always useless," he muttered.

"Never understand pirate ways. Well, gents, how's it going?"

"It'd be going faster if some people would help fill sacks instead of sitting around stuffing their faces . . . AS USUAL," Gombo said pointedly.

Marcella let out an offended squeak. "Shut up! I am not always stuffing my face! Diego, defend me!"

"There is another sack in the cabinet," Diego said diplomatically, "if you want to help."

"Well, since *you* asked *nicely*," Marcella said, jumping off the desk and flouncing over. Her dress caught on some papers on top of the desk, and they fluttered to the floor beside Diego. A strange signature on one of them caught his eye, and he set down his sack to pick up the letter. Reading it slowly, he moved over to the desk as Barbossa and Marcella joined Gombo at the chest. Marcella jostled Gombo aside and he jostled her back, and soon they were spending as much time poking each other with their elbows as they were scooping up gold coins.

Diego scanned the letter. It was written in English, but it was addressed to the admiral of the Spanish navy; evidently this had been sent on to the commander here.

> *Dear Admiral,*
>
> *I believe we can be of great use to each other, if you are interested in forming a far more lucrative partnership than the one you have now with the Pirate Lord, Captain Villanueva. I know that you, as I do, wish to eradicate pirates from the face of the globe, leaving the seas free to be ruled by powerful, eminent figures such as yourself. The destruction of the Pirate Lords is my dearest wish, and I believe that working together, we could make this*

happen soon . . . very soon.

You see, I have an army . . . the strongest army any man has ever seen. It can be summoned at a moment's notice. It does not need food, nor water, nor barracks, nor pay. It lives only to destroy. I call it my Shadow Army.

If you have any doubt of this army's power, perhaps you should pay a visit to a certain town along the Caribbean coast in Panama. Then you will know how much power I have at my fingertips.

All this power could be at your disposal. I only ask one thing: I need a ship. Do not laugh! Oh, I can hear your scoffing already. But be careful where you direct your scorn, sir. If you do not help me, then you are most certainly my enemy . . . and you do not want to be my enemy.

I am in an excellent position to betray

one of the Pirate Lords right now. When I
do this, I want your assurance that I may
keep his ship and his crew, and that you
will leave me in peace as my plan comes to
fruition. When it does, I assure you that in
return the seas will soon be cleansed of
pirates . . . forever.
  I await your response most eagerly,
  The Shadow Lord

The ink in the signature was blotchy and dark, as if the writer had pressed the pen so forcefully against the page that the ink had pooled and splattered in all directions, like a spray of blood. The handwriting was spidery and vigorous, racing wildly across the page and cramming into corners, with thin black veins skittering out from each letter. The impression was of a man quite mad. If Diego hadn't seen the devastation wrought by the Shadow Army with his own eyes, he would have dismissed the letter as the ravings of a crazed, power-hungry lunatic.

Perhaps the Spanish felt the same way—until they saw the ruins of the town. Now they must be taking this seriously. Diego wondered what their response had been. He picked up the other papers on the floor and searched the desk, but he could find nothing else that seemed related to the Shadow Lord's letter.

Still, this was important, useful information. Jack certainly ought to know about it. But if Diego took the letter, the soldiers would know that the pirates were aware of it. Perhaps it would be smarter to let them think he'd missed it. He quickly read it again and then slid the letter under a pile of other papers on the desk.

"Diego," Marcella whined. She went back to the desk, sat down in the commander's chair, and, with a pout on her face, rubbed her arms.

"My sack is too heavy. I think mine is heavier than Gombo's. It's not *fair*. I can't carry it. It makes my arms hurt."

"We're not leaving any of this behind," Barbossa said, "and you wanted to come, so now you can pull your own weight."

"*Diieeeeeego*," Marcella whined some more. He hurried over and lifted the sack she had filled, which was barely half as heavy as the other three. Wistfully, he thought of how Carolina would have carried any of these without complaining—probably all four of them, just to prove that she was strong enough.

"I can take these two," he said, lifting her sack along with his. "Let's get out of here."

"Agreed," Gombo said, standing up.

"Thank you, Diego," Marcella said sweetly, leaning her elbows on the desk, and he realized that he was only making her infatuation worse. But he didn't have much choice—they needed to get out of there quickly. Especially if there was any chance of the Shadow Lord showing up to discuss his letter.

One by one, they hefted their sacks of gold and gathered around the door. Barbossa peeked into the passageway outside.

"All clear," he whispered.

Glancing furtively around, the four of them hurried out of the fort, each feeling quite satisfied at what a surprisingly successful mission it had been.

Most satisfied of all was Marcella, although none of the others knew it.

Because back on the desk in the commander's office, a note had been secretly and hurriedly scribbled on a spare sheet of paper.

It said: *I know where you can find your precious Princess Carolina. She is on the* Black Pearl. *Come and get her.*

CHAPTER THIRTEEN

Jack edged closer to his shipmates, trying to put Jean and Carolina between him and the rather angry-looking Incan priest who was striding briskly toward them brandishing his spear. The other Incas were murmuring and pointing, and most of them were producing menacing weapons of their own. From the altar, a llama bleated nervously. Jack knew how it felt.

"How dare you interrupt the sun ceremony?" the man demanded. It was astonishing how quickly he leaped down the large stone stairs to confront them, especially since he looked to be about a hundred years old, judging by the vast system of wrinkles covering his face and his mane of silver hair. "Who are you? How did you get here?" His sharp brown eyes, bulging from under his unusually high forehead, darted among them.

"You speak English!" Jack said, surprised. "That worked out rather well, then—apart from the spear, which we would rather you pointed in a different direction."

"I'm not speaking English," the priest said. "*You're* speaking Quechua."

"Look, mate, I think I would know if I were—" Jack started, then looked down at the *quipu* in his hand. "Oh. Are you doing that, too?"

The ancient Inca's face softened when he saw the *quipu*. "Ah," he said, "I see." He leaned his golden spear against the closest stone wall and took the string reverently from Jack, running the knots through his fingers. With a smile, he said, "Tia Dalma, my old friend. Then you must be here for the Shadow Gold."

Jack was delighted. "I am indeed," he said. "I am the legendary Captain Jack Sparrow—I assume you've heard of me?"

"No," the Inca said. "But Tia Dalma's servant asked us to safeguard the gold until she sent us one who would need it. And I can see from the thick cover of shadow around you that *you* are he."

Jack shrugged, trying to hide his uneasiness. Was it really so obvious? "Well, thanks for looking after it," he said. "Lovely of you. I hope they're all this easy."

"I don't know if I would say easy," the priest said. "It's up there." He turned and pointed to a tiny mountain that rose up at the far end of the city, climbing into the clouds above the mountain peaks that surrounded it. When Jack squinted, he could see a set of horrifyingly steep stone steps carved into the side of the mountain, leading all the way to a small temple right at the very top.

"Why am I not surprised?" he said. "Of course there would be climbing." He clapped Jean on the back. "Looks like an excellent job for you, Jean. Good luck and all that. Hurry back."

"Figures," Jean said ruefully.

"I'll get it!" Carolina jumped in. "Let me— I'll run right up to the top—I swear I can!"

"No," the Incan said, shaking his head. "You must retrieve it yourself, Captain. That is Tia Dalma's instruction."

"Bossy wench," Jack said indignantly. Then he sighed. Well, at least he'd have a chance to drink the Shadow Gold before anyone could stop him.

The other inhabitants of the city followed Jack and his crew to the base of the mountain where the steps began. The wind was stronger there, and it would certainly be stronger still at the top where the temple was. Jack took off his hat and handed it reverently to Carolina.

"Do you solemnly swear to take very good care of this hat?" he asked her.

"I will," she said earnestly.

"Or else I will leave you here when the ship sails," he said. "And who knows what might happen then—that llama looks mighty hungry," he said, gesturing to the animal slumped droopily over the altar.

"Trust me," she said, holding onto the hat tightly. "I will not let anything happen to it."

"Good," Jack said. He shook Jean's hand. "Back in a moment. Don't have too much fun without me."

Jack resolutely started up the steps. At first,

they slanted up like a normal staircase, but before long they became narrower and shorter and steeper, and soon he felt as if he were climbing straight up a vertical wall—as if he would fall right off the mountain if he only tipped backward a little bit.

Beside the steps were patches of grass and rocks occasionally broken by an odd statue or a flash of fur that might have been a chinchilla or an alpaca bounding away. Jack tried not to look around too much after one very unwise glance downward. He was lucky the clouds hid the ground far below, but just the fact that they were so far below him was unsettling enough.

He clambered quickly, and the air turned chilly. He was glad he had his long coat on. He began to use his arms as well as his legs to pull himself up, although everything soon began to ache. He tried to tell himself that this was not so different from ascending up to the crow's nest, and he reminded himself of all the years he had spent clambering up ratlines and scampering up masts while dreaming of captaining his own ship.

After a long while, his hands suddenly touched open air, and he looked up, realizing that he had reached the top. The temple stood before him, open to the sky. He pulled himself up and collapsed on the cold floor slabs, catching his breath. At one end of the temple stood a curved stone altar with hollows carved in it. Resting in a hollow at the top, exactly in the path of the rising sun so that rays of light shone directly on it, was the shimmering vial of Shadow Gold.

His heart pounding with excitement, Jack scrambled to his feet and hurried over to it. He reached out to take it . . . and a sword came down, barely missing his hand and ricocheting off the stone altar with a ringing metallic sound.

Startled, Jack leaped back and beheld his attacker.

It was the Pirate Lord Villanueva.

"I see you're after my gold," he said in a menacing voice.

Jack blinked at him. "Hang on. How did you get up here?" he asked.

"I have my ways," Villanueva said mysteriously.

Jack looked around at the temple, the isolated mountaintop, and the long stretch of steep stone stairs behind him.

"No, seriously," he said, "how did you get up here?"

Villanueva looked irritated. "There's an easier path on that side," he said, waving his sword toward the far side of the mountain. "A llama brought me up."

"Well, that is unjust," Jack said. "Someone might have mentioned this easier path to me. I think I'll blame Marcella. Been looking for a reason to toss her off the crew."

"The point is," Villanueva said firmly, determined to get back to sounding menacing, "that you are trying to steal my gold."

"*Your* gold?" Jack echoed. "And what makes it yours, mate? Looks like it's just sitting there for me to take." He lunged for the vial and Villanueva brought his sword up sharply, stopping him. Jack drew his own sword and stepped back, balancing lightly on his feet.

"I know it was meant for me," Villanueva said. "My old rival, Chevalle, said that Mistress Ching has one of these vials, and I suspect he has one as well. He was gloating about it—said the best Pirate Lords have them. Which means this one must have been intended for me before it went astray."

"Perhaps it was meant for me," Jack suggested.

Villanueva sneered. "I doubt that very

much." He took a step toward the altar, and Jack deftly parried, striking the older man's sword aside and driving him back.

"You don't even know what it is," Jack said, lunging and slashing. "It's just some old shiny stuff. Probably cursed. I'd be doing you a favor, taking it off your hands." Villanueva dodged and slashed back. The crash and clang of swords echoed across the mountains.

"No one knows what it is," Villanueva said with a spinning sideswipe. "We only know that it is beautiful, and we want it." Despite his short stature and hefty bulk, the Spanish pirate was a very accomplished swordsman, nearly as skilled as Jack himself.

"Ah. That's logical," Jack said, darting aside.

"That's pirates," Villanueva responded with a shrug, and Jack certainly couldn't argue with that. He jumped back from a sharp thrust and found himself teetering at the edge of the cliff.

Windmilling his arms frantically, he was able to regain his balance—but Villanueva was already striding toward the vial.

"No!" Jack cried. "My shiny stuff!" He sprang forward, somersaulting through the air, and landed on the altar as Villanueva reached it. Quickly, Jack grabbed the vial, but Villanueva's hand wrapped around his before he could open it. Their hands locked together, they pulled, yanking the vial back and forth with furious force. Jack nearly fell off the altar, but finally he kicked Villanueva in the gut. With a grunt of pain, the Spanish Pirate Lord let go and staggered back, clutching his stomach.

Jack immediately pulled the cork off the top of the vial and poured the Shadow Gold into his mouth. As he swallowed, he felt the warmth and the pale gold energy flood through him once more. This time it felt even more powerful and intense than before. He felt rejuvenated, whole, healthy. He felt as if he could rise up and fly straight into the sun, which was beaming down on him as he stood on the altar.

Villanueva was sputtering in disbelief. "What—you—what did you—you *drank* it!" he cried. "Why would you do that? You are mad! Out of your mind. Lunatic! It was beautiful! Now it is gone!"

"Gone to a better place," Jack said cheerily. He jumped down from the altar and bowed deeply to Villanueva. "Excellent fight. Great to see you. Let's catch up again some other time. Or never, that would be fine as well." He bounded over to the steps and began to jump lightly down them, two at a time. A few steps down he paused and called back to Villanueva, "Oh, by the way—working with the Spanish, Villanueva? Don't you think that's a bit low, even for you?"

Laughing to himself at the Spaniard's

astonished expression, Jack continued down the mountain, feeling like he had wings on his feet. This Shadow Gold was amazing! If just two vials made him feel this fantastic, he couldn't wait to see what happened when he found the third.

CHAPTER FOURTEEN

The trip down the mountain was far easier and faster than the trip up. Carolina and Jean looked surprised to see Jack returning so soon.

"Wasn't it there?" Jean asked.

"Did you have trouble?" Carolina said, sounding concerned. "Do you need someone to go back up with you?"

"Not at all," Jack said, too full of joy and energy to be offended by their doubt in him. "I have the vial right here." He had wrapped the empty vial carefully inside his kerchief so the shape of it was clear, but no one could tell it was empty. He held it up and waggled it at his companions.

"Well done, Captain," the Incan priest said. "You have indeed earned the Shadow Gold, as Tia Dalma believed you would."

"Where are we going next?" Jean asked.

"A capital question," Jack said. "Any suggestions, mate?" He turned to the priest.

The old man ran the *quipu* through his fingers again. His eyes closed and he nodded, murmuring to himself. Finally he opened his eyes again and tucked the *quipu* inside his robes.

"This will help you," he said, picking up his spear and handing it to Jack. "It has the power of the sun god Inti in it."

"Oh," Jack said, hefting the spear in his hands. It was heavy and warm and reflected the sun's rays from its golden surface. But it didn't seem very strong—in fact, it reminded Jack of the time his sword had turned to silver, and then gold, back in New Orleans when he was fighting the curse of an amulet. It had been very pretty but surprisingly useless.*

Besides, a spear wasn't exactly a map to the next vial of Shadow Gold, was it?

"Very nice," he said. "Very . . . shiny. Thanks for that."

The priest escorted them back to the entrance to the tunnels. "We wish you luck in your quest," he said. His face darkened, and his eyes were full of deep sadness. "The Shadow Lord is a man much to be feared," he said. "He will bring great evil to the Seven Seas if he is not stopped. We hope you are strong enough to do so."

Jack shifted uncomfortably. That certainly

* In *Jack Sparrow*, Vols. 5, 6, and 7.

didn't *sound* like him. "Right, well, let's cross that bridge when we come to it, shall we?" He waved the other two into the cave ahead of him. "Back to the *Pearl*, sailors!"

In the cool darkness of the tunnels, the spear glowed with the same light as the *quipu*, but stronger, so they could see the rocky ceilings above them and the jagged path beneath their feet. They followed the light once more through the maze of caves until they emerged from the side of the mountain, back in the jungle where they had started, and, judging by the position of the sun, only moments after they had left.

"Well, that worked out very well, if I do say so myself," Jack said, brushing off his coat. "Not that it's unusual for a plan of mine to go smoothly, except in the sense that one never actually has before. Now all we have to do is—"

"*Aqui!*" a voice shouted behind them. "*Los piratas!*"

"I don't like the sound of that," Jack said.

They spun around to see a Spanish soldier running through the trees toward them. Quickly they turned to run in the other direction—and found a group of soldiers crashing through the bushes there.

"Right," Jack said. "Here's the plan. You distract them, I'll run."

"Yes, sir!" Carolina said, drawing a sword and leaping into an attack position.

"Where'd you get that?" Jack marveled.

"Don't worry, I'll defend you, Captain!" she cried.

"Good, excellent," Jack said. "I like this plan. Simple, easy to remember." He sprinted away with his arms flailing wildly, vanishing downhill toward the path. Jean grabbed Carolina's arm.

"He doesn't mean it!" Jean cried. "Well, I mean—he does, but don't listen to him! We should all run!"

"But shouldn't we fight?" she asked. "Shouldn't we listen to our captain?"

"Think of it this way," Jean said. "What would Jack himself do if someone gave him those orders?"

"Good point," she said, and they both turned to run after Jack.

The branches whipped at their faces and arms and legs, and roots seemed to sprout out of nowhere to catch and trip them. Behind them, pistol shots rang out, and the crashing of heavy boots through the undergrowth signaled that the soldiers were giving chase.

"I'm guessing Barbossa's plan went well," Jean gasped. "That must be why they're all out in the jungle looking for pirates."

"Wonderful!" Carolina called, dodging a thick tree trunk. "Thanks *very* much, Barbossa!"

They broke through to the path and found Jack locked in a spirited sword fight with three soldiers who were guarding the way back to the beach. He still had the Incan spear, which he was using to fend off whichever soldiers he wasn't presently sparring with. Jean and Carolina jumped into the fray, each taking one of the soldiers. Their swords clashed and clanged, driving the Spaniards back toward the fort. But each moment they were held there was a chance for the men behind them to catch up, and then they'd be far outnumbered.

"Quick!" Carolina shouted, grabbing one end of the spear from Jack. Holding the spear horizontally like a bar across them, they ran forward and drove the three Spaniards back until they all tripped and tumbled to the ground.

"Nice trick," Jack said to himself. "I should remember that."

The pirates leaped over the soldiers while they were still climbing groggily to their feet. By the time they'd figured out what had happened,

Jack, Jean, and Carolina were running as fast as their feet could carry them along the path to the beach.

They burst out of the trees onto the warm white sand and saw the *Black Pearl* already in the water with her sails raised. Barbossa was standing on the deck arguing with Diego, Billy, and Gombo.

"Clever Barbossa!" Jack cried, racing ahead. "He knew we'd have to make a quick exit, so he's all ready to go! I knew there was a reason I kept him around."

Carolina narrowed her eyes. She had a hunch Barbossa had been planning to make a "quick exit" of his own—no captain required.

They dove into the water and swam up to the ship, seizing the rope ladders that Diego and Billy threw down to them, and they swarmed up onto the deck.

"Oh, hello, Jack. We, uh . . . heard you

comin'," Barbossa, with an insincere smile on his face, said to Jack.

Distracted by the troop of men chasing them with swords, Jack didn't stop to question his first mate's intentions. "Haul anchor!" he bellowed. "To the sails! All those other things! Away at top speed! Oh, and Barbossa, it's *Captain* Jack." His men leaped into action, scurrying about like madmen.

Back on the beach, soldiers poured out of the jungle, frantically firing their muskets at the *Pearl.* But it was too late; the *Black Pearl* was already on her way out to sea, and the open horizon shone brightly ahead of the crew.

Carolina had never been so relieved. It felt like home, standing on the deck of the *Pearl.* Diego ran up and threw his arms around her, lifting her and spinning her around. From near the main mast, Marcella put her hands on her hips and glared at them.

"I was worried about you!" Diego said, setting Carolina down again. He thought she looked even wilder and more beautiful than she had when he'd left her a few short hours ago.

She laughed. "I think I have more reason to worry about *you*. You left half the Spanish army thrashing around in the jungle looking for us! Very smooth, Diego!" She punched his arm.

"*Si*, they're not very pleased with us," he said. "We may have relieved them of a few gold coins." He flipped one into her hand, and she held it up admiringly.

"*Hermosa*," she said happily. "Isn't being a pirate fun, Diego?"

"But it's also dangerous," he said, lowering his voice. "I found a letter from the Shadow Lord. He sounds like a monster—Carolina, I'm not sure it's safe to be sailing with one of the Pirate Lords, when someone so powerful hates them all so much. I would . . . I would hate for anything to happen to you."

"So would I," she said. "For instance, I would hate to marry a man I don't love or be forced to live in a fort doing embroidery for the rest of my days. Being a pirate and fighting an evil man sounds much better than that, doesn't it?" She squeezed his hand. "Besides, at least this way we're together, right?"

He couldn't help smiling. "That is true."

"Oh, Dieeeeego," Marcella called from across the ship. "Could you help me figure out how to work this?" She held up the spyglass and pouted.

Carolina laughed. "Your lady summons you," she said playfully to Diego.

With a sigh, he climbed up to where Marcella was standing at the stern of the ship. They had sailed out of the cove and were speeding along the coast of South America, heading east. Black storm clouds were beginning to gather in the evening sky; it looked like it was going to be a rough night.

"I just can't figure this thing out at all," Marcella said, tapping Diego on the chest with the spyglass. "It's soooo *complicated.*"

"Not really," Diego said, holding it up to his eye. "You just look through here—" He broke off suddenly, staring fixedly at the sea behind them.

"Oh, through *that* end?" Marcella said. "My goodness, I thought it was the other end! No wonder it didn't work! Oh, I'm *so silly,* that didn't even *occur* to me. I *wish* I were as clever as *you* are, Diego—"

"Captain Sparrow!" Diego shouted. "Captain Sparrow, quick!"

Jack sprang up the steps beside him. "Oh, what is it, now, mate?"

Diego handed him the spyglass, although at

this point they didn't need it to see the sail in the distance, rapidly closing in on them. "I think it's the same ship, sir," he said. "The one that followed us from New Orleans."

Jack frowned. He'd been sure they'd lost that ship. Who could they be? Whoever they were, they were awfully determined. Was it Villanueva? But he wouldn't have been in New Orleans—and he couldn't have gotten to South America as quickly as the *Pearl* if he'd been behind them. Perhaps it was more Spaniards searching for Carolina. Or could it be someone looking for Jack?

If only it were someone looking for Marcella. That wouldn't be so bad, Jack reflected. Whoever it was could certainly have Marcella.

"Alex," Jack said, "take the wheel and aim for those islands up ahead. We'll try to lose them in there. Savvy?"

"Aye-aye, Captain Jack Sparrow," the zombie

said, going obediently to the wheel.

"And then sail away *north*, right, Jack?" Billy said. "That is to say, in the direction of *North Carolina?*"

"Billy, I hardly think this is the time for nitpicking about maps and things," Jack said. "We're in the middle of a high-speed chase, hadn't you noticed?" He hurried off to give orders to the rest of his crew, and Billy Turner sighed heavily.

The wind whipped past, getting stronger with the approaching storm as the *Pearl* sailed up to a group of small green islands, rocky and tall enough to hide them from view, if they could get far enough ahead of the pursuing ship.

Carolina paced the deck anxiously, watching the sail behind them. What would Jack do if they ordered him to give her up? What would he do if they offered him money? She guessed he wouldn't have a hard time choosing between her and a pile of gold coins. But she would not go back to *San Augustin*. No matter what she had to do.

"There!" Jack called to Alex. "Aim between those two islands that are close together—we'll sneak around the other side while they're still coming through the channel."

The tall cliffs rose up on either side of them as the *Pearl* sailed between the two islands.

And then they noticed—there weren't two islands.

It was one island, curved in a crescent shape around a small bay, with only the narrow channel providing an exit.

"Just kidding!" Jack called. "Go back! Back, back, back!"

But it was too late. Before they could turn around completely, the other ship was looming up in the gap behind them. They were trapped.

"Oh, very clever, Jack," Barbossa sneered.

"Completely intentional, I assure you," Jack responded blithely. "All part of my brilliant plan."

"And if I might inquire, what are the other parts?" Barbossa demanded.

"I'm still working on those," Jack admitted.

The unknown ship sailed closer and closer. It was not Villanueva's galleon, the *Centurion*. It did not fly a pirate flag. Nor did it fly a Spanish flag. In fact, no banner at all fluttered from the top mast. It was an eerie, mysterious ship wreathed in the mist of the gathering storm, approaching like a faceless man in a dark alley.

The pirates all drew their swords. They manned the cannons. They stood with pistols in hand, ready to fight whoever—or whatever—was approaching them.

CHAPTER FIFTEEN

The other ship did not fire. It glided slowly, closer and closer, edging through the narrow gap between the cliffs and approaching the *Black Pearl* like a silent ghost.

"Captain Sparrow," Diego said, peering through the spyglass again. "Look at this."

Jack aimed the spyglass at the other ship. He saw a man with dark skin standing at the bow, waving a white flag. They wanted Parlay!

"That's odd," Jack said. "They chased us a long way just to have a chat."

"I say we blow them out of the water," Barbossa snarled.

"Of course you do," Jack said dismissively. "Billy, wave the white flag back. Let's hear what they have to say."

Barbossa stomped off, grumbling, as Jack and Billy held up the white flag, signaling their agreement to meet peacefully. Jack sent Alex and the others to drop the anchor, and they waited as the other ship slowly sailed up beside them.

"Hello!" the man at the bow called. Several other men gathered by the rail beside him. They all had gleaming black skin and strong muscles. "We are looking for someone, and we believe he is aboard your ship!"

"Marcus?" said a voice behind Jack. Jack turned and saw Gombo climbing up beside him. The cook was blinking in disbelief, and a great smile began to spread across his face. "Marcus, you escaped! You all did! The gods be praised!"

"Thanks to you!" Marcus called back. "Gombo, we burned the plantation and stole his ship and came looking for you. We want you to be our captain!"

"Oh, too bad, mates," Jack interjected. "I'm afraid he's already got a job. As our cook. I'm sure he wouldn't want to give that up."

"Me?" Gombo said in surprise, ignoring Jack. "Are you sure? You want me to be captain of the *Ranger*?"

"We know you'd be a better captain—and a better leader—than our former master," Marcus responded. "You were the one who led us to freedom. You're a hero, sir. We couldn't serve under anyone else. That's why we've been chasing you all this time. We thought we'd never catch you!"

Gombo took a deep breath. The bright

whiteness of his enormous smile seemed to light up the lowering dusk. "I would be honored to be your captain," he said, and a great cheer went up from the escaped slaves on the other ship.

"Are you sure you'd rather be a captain than stay here with us and cook that magnificent jambalaya?" Jack said wistfully.

Gombo smiled knowingly. "Thank you, Captain Sparrow," Gombo said, taking Jack's hand and shaking it warmly. "I won't forget how you helped me."

"Well, if you must go, a word of advice," Jack said, leaning closer, with a wise expression on his face. "You can't be a captain with a name like 'Gombo.' Lacks a certain dignity, if you will. Makes a fellow hungry, not terrified. Savvy?" He narrowed his eyes and nodded meaningfully.

"I will take *his* name," Gombo said with steely resolve. "My former master's. He stole my life—my name, my identity, my family. Now I will take his. No one shall remember who he was. There will be only one Gentleman Jocard . . . and it is *I*."

Jack and the rest of his crew stood at the rail waving good-bye as Captain Jocard was rowed to his ship by his enthusiastic crew. Jack felt a pang of jealousy. He wished he had a crew that would follow him across the whole Caribbean trying to get him to be their captain. Pirates—they never knew what was good for them.

"Good riddance," Marcella said petulantly, crossing her arms. "He didn't even say good-bye. Pirates!"

"Remarkable," Billy said. "Gentleman Jocard, newest pirate captain in the Caribbean."

"Yes," Jack said. "I've a feeling we'll be seeing him again."

Dark had fallen. A gale was howling around the *Pearl*, but inside the captain's cabin it was quiet and warm. Candlelight illuminated a map of the world spread out on the table in the center of the room. Gathered around the table were Jack's friends. And Marcella.

"What's the next step, Jack?" Jean asked. "Where do we go from here?"

"As far away from Spain as possible," Carolina voted. The day's chase had given her quite a scare.

"I agree," Diego said.

"Well, I hope wherever we go it's civilized," Marcella snapped, fanning herself.

"What about North Carolina?" Billy demanded.

"Yes, yes. Of course, Billy my mate. We just have one more stop to make first," Jack said, spinning a globe beneath his hands. "But don't worry, it's on the way."

"I want to see this Shadow Gold, if we're going to spend so much time a-hunting it," Barbossa said suspiciously.

"It's quite safe, I assure you," Jack said with a

sly smile. "No danger of anyone else stealing it from us. You can be sure of that."

"Wherever Captain Jack Sparrow wants to go, we should do that," Alex intoned, staring blankly into space.

"Now that's the spirit!" Jack said happily. He clapped the zombie on the back with a grin, then quickly pulled his hand away and wiped it off on his thigh. "Don't worry," he went on. "I have a plan."

Jean laughed. "Usually that's *exactly* when we *do* have to worry."

Jack trailed his fingers across the map on the table. "It so happens that I know who has one of the vials . . . and I know where to find her." He tapped the map meaningfully, and they all leaned in closer to peer at what he was pointing at. Barbossa sighed.

"China?" Carolina said excitedly. "We're going to China? *Santa Maria*, we're going to meet Mistress Ching!" she said to Diego.

"Ew, *China*," Marcella said scornfully. "I hear they eat with sticks, instead of forks like *civilized* people."

"That is definitely NOT 'on the way' to North Carolina," Billy objected.

"Just this one stop!" Jack said. "Not to worry! Man the sails, me hearties. We're off to Asia!"

EPILOGUE

Dear Sir,

We have received your proposal, and we find ourselves in complete agreement with you: ridding the seas of the plague of pirates, particularly those who call themselves "Lords" of the "Brethren Court," is of the utmost importance. Moreover, your offer of such a powerful army is most enticing. It seems that with such mutual goals and priorities, working together would clearly

be of mutual benefit. Therefore, we hereby
agree to your proposal, and when you have
betrayed the Pirate Lord of whom you
speak, we will not hinder you in your quest
to destroy all the others as well.

Godspeed

The letter was signed by a Spanish admiral. The imprint of his seal beside the signature glowed in the candlelight as the Shadow Lord examined the parchment carefully.

Beyond the circle of candlelight loomed stacks of barrels and shelves laden with rum bottles, webbing to hold the cargo in place, and in the dark far corner of the hull, the jail cells that awaited any who crossed the captain. The floorboards rose and fell beneath his feet as the ship slammed across the waves, battling the fierce winds of the storm outside.

The Shadow Lord smiled. Of course the Spanish had accepted his offer. They must have learned what he'd done in Panama. The prospect of having the most powerful army in the world at their side was too much to resist. And he had carefully avoided mentioning exactly *which* Pirate Lord he was going to betray first.

A shadow curled up from the floor below him and wound around his hand. He caressed it absentmindedly like a cat, letting it circle through his fingers and press itself against his ring as if yearning to join the other shadows inside.

The Shadow Lord folded the letter and replaced it safely inside his coat. Little did the Spanish admiral know what the Shadow Lord had planned for his Shadow Army. Once he had defeated the Pirate Lords, it was a natural step from there to conquering all the armies of the world—all the ships that sailed on all the oceans, from the freezing poles to the blistering equatorial seas. All of it would be his. Finally the world would know his power, and then they would respect him. Soon his day would come.

But first . . . he had a Pirate Lord to kill.

Don't miss the next thrilling volume of

DISNEY
PIRATES of the CARIBBEAN

LEGENDS OF THE BRETHREN COURT

Rising in the East

Jack and his crew are off to China. But before Jack can secure more Shadow Gold he'll need to fight off the Pirate Lords Mistress Ching and Sao Feng, *and* the East India Trading Company. Can even *Jack* survive such a terrible triangle?